Also by Paul Zindel

Raptor

Rats

Other titles available from Hodder Children's Books

THE STONEHEART TRILOGY

Stoneheart

Ironhand

Silvertongue

Charlie Fletcher

THE DEAD

The Dead

The Dark

The Damned

David Gatward

BATS

PAUL ZINDEL

Hodder
Children's
Books

A division of Hachette Children's Books

To Isabel Boissier

CONTENTS

EMERGENCE

Jake heard the small mammal sounds erupting from the end of the high ramp where the vines swirled to form a cave. There came the flutter of wings, and the nightly Emergence had begun: a blanket of glistening bats – hundreds of bats! – with bulldog-like ears and tiny faces that looked like they had been punched in.

Bats flying right at Jake.

Jake called down from the canopy to his dad, on the jungle floor. 'Send the sling up for me. Now, Dad, *now.*'

He tried to escape, but it was too late. The wave of bats swelled and began to wash up over his legs. They bit at his ankles, small razor cuts from short, feeding jaws.

'Help me! Dad!' he shrieked.

Jake drew in air to scream. A living, furry scarf scampered up to cover his mouth. One of the bats tore at his lips, then shimmied its small hairy head and legs and wing tips inside of his mouth. He tried to yell as it crawled violently, deep into his throat.

A small head.

Biting inside him.

Jake screaming. Screaming and praying and...

'Wake up, young man. Excuse me. Wake up.'

Jake Lefkovitz's eyes snapped open. He realized that the flight attendant was shaking him by the shoulder.

'Oh... sorry,' Jake said, bolting upright in his

window seat on the M-80 jetliner.

'Please put your seat forward and make certain your safety belt is secure,' the flight attendant said. She smiled. 'We'll be landing in Manaus in twenty minutes.'

Jake noticed several of the passengers were staring at him. He knew he must have cried out. The remnants of the nightmare were like snakes turning in the back of his mind. 'I dreamed my allowance got cut,' he announced, laughing and rapping his knuckles on his head like a clown.

He knew he had stayed up too long the night before. For weeks, he'd spent hours at the New York Public Library reading like a demon, everything he could get his hands on about bats and the Amazon. He'd read books and magazines from the Smithsonian. A colleague of his father's had lent him videos and audio tapes from the Museum of Natural History. One was about batologists like his father, working high in the rainforest canopy of Brazil. The other was about the wildlife – capybaras, deadly anacondas. Army ants cutting a ten-foot swath through the jungle.

On this trip, Jake was determined to prove himself to his dad, who thought Jake couldn't take anything seriously. It was true that he had a reputation as a joker, that he liked a good laugh. Now he wanted to show he had grown up and changed – that he could be part of his father's research team and act responsibly.

Jake looked out the plane window as it circled low over Manaus, the capital of the Amazonas state. From the air it appeared to be an oasis of broad streets and plazas in the middle of a belt of greedy jungle – part of a lush wilderness territory as big as the United States. When the plane landed, the flight attendant kept her eye on him.

'I'm OK,' Jake said. 'I always yell when I sleep.'

'How strange,' the flight attendant said.

His face reddened. He covered his embarrassment with a wink as he got his over-stuffed duffle bag, a heavy cardboard box bound with rope, and a big aluminium stereo down from a storage compartment. He put a small bag of peanut butter cookies saved from the in-flight dinner into the duffle bag. Peanut butter cookies had always been his favourite and they were, by far, the best thing about the meal. He lugged his carry-ons to the open doorway, where the heat socked into him like a hammer.

As he came down the stair ramp, it was easy for him to spot the guide his father had sent to meet him. A tiny, wrinkled man with waist-length grey hair waited alone on the Tarmac.

'Welcome to Manaus, Master Jake,' the man said as he extended his hand. 'I'm Hanuma, your father's foreman.'

'Ciao,' Jake said, taking Hanuma's thin stiff

hand and shaking it. ' "Ciao" is Italian for hello and goodbye.'

'I see.' Hanuma stared at him and took his hand back. 'I have a taxi waiting to take us to the river dock,' he said, leading the way through the stifling, small terminal and out an exit to the pick-up area.

'Did you ever find the missing men from the expedition?' Jake asked.

'No...'

'It's a little scary, isn't it? When Dad called last week, he sounded really worried about them. Is it possible they just got bored and took off?'

Hanuma grunted. 'My workers do not *take off*,' he said. 'The missing men are the main reason Dr Lefkovitz didn't want you to come out to the camp. He said you should stay in Manaus and he can join you down here at the end of the month. See the theatro. The museums. There would be time for a safe tour of the river

6

before the rains came.'

'No way,' Jake said. 'I'm going back upriver with you guys. Dad's been gone too long. If something weird is going on out at his camp, I don't want him doing a disappearing act either. Guys don't just disappear from my dad's expeditions. Even my Mom's worried and wants him to pack it in.'

'Then why didn't she come?'

'Well, she's with a law firm and is still busy clawing her way to the top. Last week her company sent her to Tonga. I don't even know where that is.'

'That explains it,' Hanuma said.

'What?'

'Why you are in Manaus despite your father's warning. You just do whatever you want.' Hanuma smiled, flashing a gold front tooth.

Jake laughed. 'Yeah, sort of. Except when Dad's around. You probably get tired of doing everything he says, too. I'll bet he's got *all* you guys jumping through hoops. He loves to do that.'

Hanuma glanced up toward the equatorial sun. 'Ah, I understand you now. You need to be someone important. I think you want your father to see that you have learned to be wise and have courage. My seventeen sons and daughters were like you when they were young. Full of themselves. Maybe you will learn as your father has that sometimes, in the Amazon,' he said seriously, 'it is a fine thing if one can jump *very* high.'

'Maybe.'

'Oh, it's true,' Hanuma said. 'Or it can be "Ciao, baby" forever.'

THE RIVER

*T*he taxi driver, a young Indian wearing a grime-stained baseball cap and a T-shirt, left the side of his beat-up Ford station wagon, and helped Jake put his luggage into the trunk. Jake kept his CD player with him.

'What is in the big cardboard box?' Hanuma asked Jake.

'Some electrical thingamajig. I did my science project on echolocation – bat radar. Some pretty interesting stuff. I figured Dad would want to see it.'

'Perhaps,' Hanuma said, as he and Jake slid into the back seat. 'Those are nice Gap jeans and a Tommy shirt you have on.'

'Thanks,' Jake said. 'You sound like you've been to the States a lot.'

'Enough to know that an air-conditioned mall is more fun than the jungles of Juruá Lace. And safer.'

'Safer I don't know about,' Jake said. 'We've got our share of savages running around Manhattan too, you know. How long's the trip to Dad's camp?'

'A small moon and fourteen waterfalls.'

'Is that like half past a jaguar's a—?'

Hanuma cut him off. 'Dr Lefkovitz warned me that you would be a very silly boy.'

'Thank you. I *am* the only one in our family that still has a sense of humour.'

'If that's what you want to call it,' Hanuma

said. 'Dr Lefkovitz says you can be a real teenage pain in the butt.'

'How's that for PR?'

Hanuma sighed.

As the taxi left the center of Manaus, the elaborate fountains and statues of the plazas gave way to narrow streets of makeshift Indian stores and checkerboard gardens. Several tourist cafés with striped awnings and neon signs lined the riverbank near the main deep water dock. Gaudy tour boats were moored side by side small fishing skiffs and beached narrow dugouts called pirogues.

The driver pulled the taxi to a halt at one of the small Indian docks. Two well-built men in loincloths left their freshly-stocked pirogue and helped Jake with his duffle bag and box of rattling electronics. Jake held tight to his stereo.

By the time Hanuma had finished haggling with the driver over the fare, the men were ready to launch the pirogue on to the river.

Jake knew his father had sent his best men to bring him upriver: Hanuma and two Indians who had made the journey many times. They ordered Jake to sit behind Muras, the bowman with the supplies. Behind Jake was Hanuma's main man, Dangari. Hanuma squatted at the back of the pirogue where he could help rudder. Jake knew from his father's letters that Hanuma was able to troubleshoot most of his expedition's problems. He'd once been a shaman in the Murdaruci tribe, and was said to have special gifts, like clairvoyance.

'He knows across great distances, without phone or walkie-talkie, when one of his men or children has been bitten by a snake or fallen from a tree,' Dr Lefkovitz had written. 'That is why the workers missing from the camp are of great concern to us. Hanuma believes something bad has happened to them. He can no longer feel their spirits.'

Muras and Dangari were like most of the men from the Murdaruci tribe, olive-skinned, short, but with powerful builds and lustrous straight black hair like that of cliff divers. Under Hanuma's orders, they cut their paddles with the sharpness of knives into the dark river water, and used them to steer in the rapids. On the first day there was always the distant sound of screeching chain-saws and roaring earth-movers. Swaths of mahogany rainforest were being cleared as far as the eye could see. Lumber trucks with poisonous fumes coughing from their cab pipes tore along dirt roads like ruthless juggernauts.

As dusk set in, the sky reddened and the banks along a tributary of the river were unspoiled jungle again. Hanuma picked their camping spot for the night and supervised the raising of the tents and the making of a fire. Dinner was slicings from a slab of salted tapir.

The next morning, Jake helped shove off into

rapids that threatened to capsize the pirogue. At each waterfall, he pitched in with the Indians to carry the long dugout and supplies carefully up to the next stretch of flat, slower river. When it was calm, Jake played rock CDs on his stereo – and once, some loud rap just to see the look on Hanuma's face.

'I see you are trying to drive me and the jungle crazy,' Hanuma said.

'Oh, you mean the music?' Jake asked.

'Yes. The racket.'

A constant mist drifted down through the towering trees and walls of vines. The main waters of the entire Amazon basin were born in the Andes. Soon, when the high mountain snows melted, they would violently flood the area as they did every year.

'How much time before the flooding starts at the camp?' Jake asked.

'Soon,' Hanuma said. 'Maybe a couple of

weeks. The waters will rise quickly and fish will swim in the forest,' Hanuma said, his voice gentle with a mix of Portuguese and Indian accents. 'Within a month, giant water ferns will arise where your father's camp now stands. There will be too many piranha to keep away with the sound of his old truck motor. River dolphins have begun to play near the camp falls, and the spider monkeys are already chattering nervously. Yes, the high water is coming.'

'Has Dad collected a lot of nifty bats?' Jake asked.

'Plenty, if you ask me. He always wants to find more. He makes Muras draw them. Muras can draw very well.'

'Dad told me he's after vampires on this trip,' Jake said. 'They're really nasty little suckers, aren't they?'

'Yes,' Hanuma said.

'I've seen them in the nocturnal room at the

Bronx Zoological Gardens,' Jake said. 'The staff puts out Petri dishes of cow's blood for them to lap up.'

'The north jungle has many of the "little suckers", as you say, that your father wants to study,' Hanuma said. 'They sleep in the vines and hollowed tree trunks during the day. At night, they fly to feast on the backs of monkeys and wild boars. My men wake up sometimes to see bats drinking blood from their own legs and faces.'

'In that case, I guess there won't be much sack time for me.' Jake remembered his dream on the plane, and his stomach tightened. Perhaps he'd read too much about bats. The gentle way they bite. How they can give someone a fatal disease without them even knowing.

'Isn't anyone afraid of getting rabies?'

'That is a danger, too,' Hanuma said. 'You go crazy. It is a terrible death. But my men are more afraid of a puma attack or cayman alligators grabbing them in the river and eating them. Here the alligators kill and hide their prey beneath mounds of underwater peat.'

The idea was disturbing to Jake, but he had no intention of showing fear. 'Great marinade,' he said.

'My tribesmen are also afraid of evil tree spirits and mountain lightning – and tiny barbed catfish that can swim up into their body cavities.'

Jake decided not even to think about that at all.

It was afternoon by the time they reached Dark Angel Falls. Jake helped carry the pirogue and supplies up the towering, steep rocky bank to a cove above the falls. In the last hours of the journey, the river had narrowed to less than a hundred feet wide and its water became clear. Electric eels and iridescent neon fish flashed in the eddies. A jaguar watched them from high in a tree as they passed. Tapirs and capybaras drank at the river bank.

Jake noticed spider webs with strands as thick as cord. Once, when the pirogue had to pass under an overhang of tropical willows, ticks the size of acorns and large, clawed beetles rained down and had to be brushed into the river.

As the sun began to set, Hanuma called out, 'There's your father.'

STRANGERS

Jake could hardly recognize the man waiting for them in the mist at the landing. His dad looked thinner than Jake had ever seen him. It was always a shock to see him after he'd spent a few months in the jungle. By now he had a full beard, and his eyes were puffy. He wore a tan pith helmet to shield his balding head. There were always changes inside, too. Changes in the way he thought. Secrets from each expedition.

A handful of Indian workers flanked Dr

Lefkovitz on the small area that had been cleared at the riverbank. They helped beach the pirogue. As Jake disembarked he could see the camp wasn't much larger than a baseball diamond that had been carved out of the heavy foliage and giant grandilora and mahogany trees of the rainforest.

Three huts and a half dozen thatched lean-tos had been erected in a circle. Clusters of ropes and pulleys spiralled skyward as though the entire camp were controlled by the strings of a puppet master.

'I wish you hadn't come, son,' was the first thing out of Dr Lefkovitz's mouth. He extended his hand like he was greeting a stranger.

For a moment, Jake surprised himself with his own sudden anger. He realized he wanted to yell at his father, *Are those the only words you can think to say to me? You haven't seen me in months, and that's what you've got to say!*

'Pops, I know you don't want me hanging around here,' Jake said. 'You never want me on any of your bat treks.'

'If you could ever take anything seriously,' his father said, seeing the CD player Jake clutched like a suitcase.

'Dad, I've spent the last couple of months studying bats. I'll know what you're talking about. This time I can help. I'll move equipment. Build huts. I'm stronger. I was on the track and gymnastic teams at Dalton. I ran in Central Park. Worked out at the gym. You'll see...

'Jake, what I need you to be is a team player. The men won't accept a selfish fool on this expedition.'

'I'm not a selfish fool,' Jake said. 'Not anymore.'

Muras and Dangari brought Jake's things to the main hut. Hanuma gave Jake his cardboard box. 'Your son did well on the journey here,' Hanuma told Dr Lefkovitz.

Dr Lefkovitz frowned.

'What's the downer now?' Jake said, afraid that it would be the same as always – that his father wouldn't even try to see all the ways he had changed.

Jake said, 'Dad, I've got good instincts. I know how to listen to them now. Hey, I come from great genes. You're as smart as they come, and a lot of it has rubbed off on me. Just give me a chance.'

Dr Lefkovitz turned away from him and went to a crude control board radiating electric cables, and threw a switch. Two hundred feet above the camp, the jungle canopy lit up – long strings of naked light bulbs lining each of the dozens of aerial walkways and rope bridges that spread out from a central high platform like the support spokes of a circus tent. A gasoline truck motor, reclaimed from an abandoned gold mining operation, chugged away driving a crude generator at the edge of the river.

'The only way you can help around here is to keep out of our way.'

'OK, Dad,' Jake said. He'd long ago learned it was easier to *yes* his father than argue. He'd always soften after a while, and usually forget anything harsh that he'd said. 'I will,' Jake went on. 'I'll stay on the ground. I'll wash laundry. Anything. I don't care. I'll become the best worker you've got. You'll be glad I came.' Jake's gaze was fixed skyward to the dangling walkways and lights, to the high-wire glitter show – an adventure he knew he had no intention of missing.

The jungle became a wall of night by the time Jake had stowed his things. The camp itself was still ablaze from the garlands of light bulbs. Jake's bed, in the largest hut, was on the other side of the room from his father's. They were separated by a towering rack of formaldehyde jars brimming

23

with vampire bat specimens. Dozens of small mouths were agape and distorted. A sky of small black, dead eyes appeared to stare down at him. Jake hated the way scientists killed hundreds, if not thousands, of creatures just to add them to their collection. He never forgot an experiment one of his father's colleagues did once on mice. He put electrodes into the brains of living mice, and then decapitated the mice to check on how their nervous systems worked. Jake had had nightmares for months when he'd heard about that project.

There came the sound from a bamboo flute, loud and shrill. And Dr Lefkovitz's voice: 'Hey, Jake – get out here for dinner.'

'Coming,' Jake called back.

Outside, his father, Hanuma and the dozen or so Indian workers from the camp sat cross-legged on mats that covered the ground of the communal circle.

'We start our work up in the canopy after dinner,' his father said.

'I want to go up with you,' Jake said, sitting down next to his father.

'It's too dangerous – I don't want you up there.'

'I—' Jake started, but a bowl of roast pig and plump, moist bark larvae was placed in front of him. Jake knew the thick white worms were a delicacy throughout the Amazon. He also knew the men were watching him, waiting to see what he'd do.

'Ummm,' he said, picking out one of the crispiest larvae, putting it in his mouth, and chewing on it like it was a caramel.

Hanuma and the workers smiled.

'Magyar is our cook,' Hanuma said. 'He trapped and cooked the fresh boar to celebrate your arrival.'

Jake looked at the small Indian across from him,

the one smiling and nodding his head at him.

'Thank you, Magyar,' Jake said. He grabbed a piece of the wild pig and tasted it. There were softer, moist clumps clinging to it. Magyar spoke excitedly as Jake realized how tasty the clumps were.

'He wants you to know the boar was stuffed and wrapped with masticated water snake.'

'He's spoiling me,' Jake said.

Hanuma laughed loudly.

'Dad, I want you to see this gadget I made.' Jake opened his equipment box and took out a jerry-rigged power belt with a cluster of wires that looked like the kind used to hook up a DVD player. He tightened the belt around his waist, reached back into the box, and hooked up a screen and circuit board he'd adapted from an old games console.

'I can't give it any time now,' his father said. 'Maybe tonight after work. I remember last year's science fair project. You made that electronic kitty litter box – the one where the top lifted when anything crossed in front of an electric eye. And it did something when the lid closed.'

'Gave a spray of perfume.'

'Yes. It almost scared our cat to death.'

'Hey, I was only fooling around,' Jake said. 'This year I did something serious on bat flight and communication.'

'We'll see,' his father said. He brushed flecks of charred meat from his lap, and stood up. The men got to their feet and headed for the rope ladders. Dangari and Muras sat in the two-man sling elevator. It looked like a parachute harness with a swing seat. They threw a switch to engage the power shaft that had been geared to the truck engine. The sling jerked upward, lifting the men quickly to the central canopy platform.

'Pops, I want to go up,' Jake said.

His father frowned again.

Hanuma spoke up. 'The riverwalk of the canopy needs repairing. Can you tie knots?' he asked Jake.

'I'm the best knot-tie expert in the world,' Jake answered quickly. 'I was an Eagle Scout.'

Dr Lefkovitz stared at Hanuma a moment, then smiled. 'All right,' he told Jake. 'You can help reinforce the walkways. Hanuma will show you how to use the vines. The rest of us will be collecting specimens on the north walkway tonight.'

The empty sling was sent back down. Dr Lefkovitz and one of the other workers got into it and went up.

'We'll be next,' Hanuma said.

'I could climb,' Jake said. 'I only fell twice in gym class – that's because it was a single rope and I had to climb using only my hands.'

'This canopy is two hundred feet high – it's

not your gym class ceiling,' Hanuma said. 'You would fall only *once* here.'

THE CANOPY

*W*hile Dr Lefkovitz and Magyar travelled up to the canopy, Jake shook out a shoulder pouch he'd packed and put his echolocation device into it. The sling arrived back down, and Jake sat in it with Hanuma. Jake gasped as the seat jerked up into the air like the harness of a rising parachute.

'Hey, this is high,' Jake said, as they lifted quickly to the canopy platform. The central platform itself was an octagonal-shaped scaffold that circled near the top of the tallest mahogany tree. His father and the other workers had already started out along the rope bridges and slatted track of the north walkway.

Hanuma pointed to a walkway to the left that appeared to end at a wall of thick vines and foliage. 'That is the riverwalk,' Hanuma said. He led Jake to a spot high above the bank of the river. 'Your father started collecting here three months ago when we arrived, but the canopy was too thick above the river. Unyielding. It is a barrier because the mist of the river rises and feeds the jungle above it more than any other area.'

Jake set his shoulder pouch down on the walkway. 'So where do I tie knots?'

Hanuma sat down cross-legged on the walkway, and grabbed a thin, strong vine from the edge of the walkway. He took the machete hanging from his waist and sliced the vine into lengths as long as his arm.

'You tie the slats together,' Hanuma said. 'We use bow knots. Do you know bow knots?'

'Sure,' Jake said. 'Bow knots were my speciality when I was an Eagle.'

'Good,' Hanuma said, smiling. 'Up here it is excellent to be an eagle.'

Jake watched Hanuma make the first tie. The old vine-ties were frayed, rotting. Hanuma placed the new vine over the old, and tied the knots so one of the slats of the walkway was firmly attached to the other.

'Like *that*,' Hanuma said.

'Right,' Jake said.

Jake sat down across from Hanuma, then selected a piece of fresh cut vine and bound together the pair of slats in front of him. With his father and the other men gone, he could hear the sounds of insects and monkeys in the canopy. One area had been hacked away enough so Jake could glimpse the river flowing below.

Hanuma gave Jake his machete. 'Cut back the overgrowth, but don't sever the rope railings,' he said. 'Be careful.'

Jake swung the machete, and the vines and young branches gave way bit by bit. Once they had worked their way further out over the river itself, Jake knew that if the fall to the river didn't kill him, the piranha would.

'What do you think happened to the two missing workers?' Jake asked. 'I mean, what do you *really* think?'

'No one knows,' Hanuma said. 'They were working here on the riverwalk the night they disappeared. That was almost two weeks ago. They finished with the rest of us, and went down.'

Jake looked more carefully at the wall of jungle that lay ahead on the riverwalk. A coolness rose up from the river far below. 'How do you know for sure that they didn't run away?'

'We searched around the camp. There were no footprints, no signs that anyone had left the camp in any direction.'

'Maybe they left on the river.'

Hanuma took his machete back to cut several more strips of tough vine. 'No pirogues were missing. They couldn't have swum very far because of the piranha.'

Jake tied another set of the planks together.

'Did anyone see them climb down or use the sling?'

'No.'

Jake winked at Hanuma. 'I thought you were supposed to be clairvoyant? That you could feel things. See things that were happening elsewhere?'

'I don't have good feelings about the disappearance of these men, but I've chosen to hope and pray to the Great Spirit that they are still alive.'

'Well, I've been thinking about them, too,' Jake said, 'ever since Dad called and told us. I've been having bad dreams. Usually, it's because I eat too much popcorn before going to bed. But I've had these dreams about the men, and bats coming after me – and about a dozen other horrible Amazon bugs and critters I've read about. Since I was in the third grade, I've had a recurring dream that one day I'll be devoured alive.

'There was always something I was afraid of. Once, for school, I researched all the documented shark attacks in the world since recorded history. I had nightmares about sharks for years,' Jake said. He looked around at the shadows in the canopy. 'Did you ever think that maybe the missing men were still up here in the canopy? Did you ever consider that?'

Hanuma glanced uneasily towards the barrier of vines and branches. 'The men had been ordered to clear the riverwalk,' he said.

Jake took the machete back and chopped carefully at the next cluster of the green wall. A tightness began to crawl into his stomach and he could feel his pulse quickening.

'If a jaguar had taken them, we would have heard screams. A jungle cat would silence only one man at a time,' Hanuma said.

'I know jaguars bite the throat and cut off your breathing,' Jake said.

'Yes, that is the way they kill. They are merciful – they do not eat a man alive.'

Jake reached into his shoulder pouch and pulled out his electronic device. He flicked a switch and his gadget made a high pulsing noise.

BLIP ... BLIP ...

'This is Gizmo,' Jake explained to Hanuma. 'That's what I call it.'

'Gizmo?'

'Yep.'

'What does Gizmo *do*?'

'A couple of things,' Jake said. 'The "blip" sounds it makes travel out and bounce off objects, like tree trunks and stones. Whatever. Different things have different densities and don't reflect sound waves the same.' He set Gizmo's small glowing video screen on his lap. 'The sounds come back and we see a "picture". Pictures of things in the jungle.'

'You can see *through* the jungle?'

'For a hundred feet or so. It's like the way bats send out high frequency sounds and can see in the dark. The echoes let them see shapes. Gizmo's picture makes everything black and white, more like an X-ray or the image on an oscilloscope screen.'

'They were clearing the riverwalk,' Hanuma said. 'The men...'

The coolness rising from the river was now almost a chill. 'Exactly where?'

'*There.*'

Jake aimed the directional disc of the device so it pointed straight at the spot Hanuma was indicating.

BLIP...

The sounds went out and were reflected back. Images danced on the small game screen. 'You can see motion on this thing,' Jake said. 'I mean, it's hard to see the definite shape of anything – but we'll be able to look pretty deep into the canopy. You've got to train your eye.' Jake pointed out a configuration on the screen. 'See, that's a big tree trunk.'

'Your father wouldn't like you playing up here,' Hanuma said.

'Hey, this isn't play. I mean, I *won* the whole school science fair with Gizmo.' A thin, twisting image moved in the lower section of the screen. Jake felt a flush of apprehension, then recognized what it was. 'See, *that's* a snake in the canopy.'

Hanuma watched the image for a moment.

'Yes. There are many small tree pythons here,' Hanuma said. 'They are harmless, much smaller than the ordinary pythons that can crush you to death. They're not poisonous. We don't need Gizmo to tell us this.'

'Maybe your men *accidentally* fell into the river,' Jake said. 'They could have been out on a branch, and it broke off.'

'They didn't cut far enough into the overgrowth to be above the river. They would have fallen on to the bank.'

Jake put the strap of his apparatus around his neck, and stood slowly. He turned up the amplitude of the blips. Hanuma stood and looked over his shoulder.

'What is this?' Hanuma asked, pointing to a dark shape in the middle of the screen.

Jake checked it and said, 'Maybe a clump of vines.'

'Why is it moving?'

'The wind,' Jake said, but a spray of goosebumps rose on the back of his neck. 'It could be something that's alive, but it's too big. Maybe sap flowing from a hollow trunk.'

Jake used the machete and hacked deeper. With each slash, clumps of vines and branches fell away. They were farther from the lighted stretch of the riverwalk.

'We should come back with floodlights or a Coleman lamp,' Jake said hesitantly.

Hanuma watched the image of the undulating object come into focus. Near the base of it there were twisted shapes.

'Hey,' Jake said. 'It could be just a rotting branch or some kind of hive or bark maggots...'

With another powerful slash of the machete, a drape of vines dropped on to the abandoned walkway. Jake reflexively kicked the clump out of the way. In front of him was a shining bulk that swelled as high as the thick, rope railings.

The light spill rendered the mass into a sort of shroud.

'There are bones,' Hanuma said.

Jake felt a shot of adrenalin pour into his bloodstream as he gave the machete back to Hanuma, picked up a broken branch, and prodded at the centre of the form. Now he could see that whatever it was, it was covered with hundreds of tiny black, living *wings*.

ATTACK

'It's bats,' Jake said, startled. He thought about everything he'd read about them, all the pictures he'd seen in the museums' magazines. 'It's a colony of vampire bats. *Desmodus rotundus.*'

'It is more,' Hanuma said.

There was fear in Hanuma's voice, and it took Jake by surprise. Using the branch, Jake gritted his teeth as he prodded deeper into the colony. The little bats began to make high-pitched sounds, peel away from the mound, and take to the air.

They flapped away into a labyrinth of holes that had been ripped out of the underbelly of the canopy. Those bats that stayed on the heap were drinking, their tongues frantically lapping at an oozing fluid.

Hanuma said, 'They're drinking blood.'

Jake shuddered. 'COME ON, SCAT!' he yelled. He knew he had to see what dead prey was beneath them. He thought it could be a large blue heron or jungle vulture, a favourite feast for vampires. A bird could have become sick in the tree, and the vampires overwhelmed it.

But the clump was bigger. Larger and tangled.

Hanuma stepped away from the light.

They saw the oozing mass clearly now. Protruding from the top of the bloody clump were the ghastly remains of a pair of human heads, their cheeks and necks and black hair twisted and fused. Fragments of white skull glistened, and strips of light shot into holes where once there had been eyes and brains. Desiccated feet and hands and more cracked and broken bone appeared to hold the clump up, support it like the stand of a blood-soaked sculpture. The mutilated cadavers of two men, each with a shattered jaw and a mouth frozen open into a death scream.

Jake's eyes burned and his nostrils flared from the sickening stench. 'No little bats did all this,' he said, his voice breaking. But Hanuma had already turned and was heading back on the riverwalk.

There was another sound now:

BLEEP ... BLEEP ...

Jake realized he'd left Gizmo's receiver on. It was different than the blips Gizmo generated for its searching sonar. Now Gizmo was picking up the sounds of something approaching.

Coming fast.

'Hanuma,' he called. 'Wait.'

Hanuma kept moving. 'I'll get your father...'

The BLEEPS were coming closer, louder. He could hear a pulsing screech. A high pitch, as from a large bird or animal – something big crashing through the canopy. Tearing through vines and jungle.

Wings flapping.

The lights of the river ramp went out, and there was only the glowing spill from the central platform. Jake saw the image on the screen now. Something bulky, moving fast. It was thirty to forty feet to the left, tearing through the canopy and the open pockets of its underbelly. The river was two hundred feet below.

The imaged creature was past him now.

'WATCH OUT, HANUMA,' Jake called. 'IT'S HEADING TOWARD YOU.'

Hanuma heard Jake's cries. All he could think of was getting to Dr Lefkovitz. Dr Lefkovitz would know what to do. He'd know what had killed the men. What kind of evil. Hanuma felt overwhelmed by a malevolence that made his skin hot and wet. The badness of the place. A profanity. He felt the cries of the men. An evil hung in the air. Brushed against him like the hanging vines and creepers on the sides of the riverwalk. Branches scraped his arms, and caught in his long, grey hair as he ran towards the light.

Hanuma heard the hunting creature, too. The large thing racing, flapping its way through the canopy. It sounded as though it were a large puma or jaguar rapidly closing the distance between them. Bad thing. Dangerous thing. He believed he could hear spirits crying out:

Don't let it get you. Don't ...

The eruption came from the canopy wall on his left. Hanuma saw a giant bat hurl itself out at him like a winged panther. He glimpsed its claws and leathery, muscled arms. Its wings opened like a cloak of skin and its abdomen was swollen and hairy like that of an ugly, colossal moth. The creature hit into him as his brain registered clearly the enormous, wide head with large green eyes set above a squashed snout.

The impact of the giant bat knocked Hanuma down. He tried to reach for his machete, but the weapon tumbled across the walkway and over the edge. Claws locked on his shoulders like vices. Hanuma was ashamed of his scream – a scream like that of an old woman. He shrieked again, as the monstrous bat drove its two long front fangs deep into his neck. They were honed, pointed teeth plunging into Hanuma's spine. He trembled as his blood burst out on to the walkway in front of him.

Jake was stunned when the creature exploded from the canopy. He saw it seize Hanuma, biting and clawing at him viciously. The walkway shook violently, and Jake had to grab for the rope railing to stop from falling over the side and down into the river.

Whatever the beast was, Jake saw it pulling Hanuma fast towards the central platform – Hanuma sliding, his limp body moving quickly away. Jake steadied himself and started after Hanuma and the monster. The creature was dragging the old man by the neck, half-carrying him over the planks, using its wing tips like crutches – like the bats in Jake's nightmare! The giant bat was trying to haul Hanuma off into the canopy.

Into the air.

'Help! Help!' Jake called out, hoping his father would hear.

He gained ground. A hundred thoughts shot through Jake's mind at once. He thought of the power pack around his waist. He thought of Gizmo, and of just throwing himself on the creature. He'd try to stamp on its wings and make it break its grip on Hanuma.

Jake was shouting at the thing now, shouting at it like it was a bad dog: 'DROP HIM. YOU DROP HIM. YOU LET HIM LOOSE.'

SCREAMS

Dr Lefkovitz and the men heard Hanuma and the cries for help. The old shaman's screams were heart-stopping — Jake's shouts chilling. Several of the men were harvesting bat specimens from traps along a rope bridge. There was no way they could make it back quickly on to the slatted stretch of the northwalk.

Along with Dangari and Muras, Dr Lefkovitz reacted as if he'd heard a bomb go off. The frightened men turned back, moving as fast as they dared on the aerial walkway.

Jake, his father thought, *what if he's fallen! What if he or Hanuma has fallen!*

Near the central platform, the northwalk angled and ran parallel to the riverwalk. The first Dr Lefkovitz could see of Hanuma was across the gulf between the catwalks. His body was sliding as if by magic, a limp doll nearly airborne, grasped in the jaws of a darkness.

Dr Lefkovitz gasped. 'Oh, my God.'

Closer, he saw the shape of the shadowy thing, retreating with its spoils. The lights on the riverwalk were out. Hanuma's body was being carried headfirst now, his face raised so that his eyes stared up into the snarling mouth of the beast.

Dangari and Muras slowed, trembled. Dr Lefkovitz saw them holding back.

'COME ON,' he ordered.

Suddenly, Jake burst from the shadows of the

riverwalk, racing to save Hanuma. Jake was on instinct now. He had turned up the volume on Gizmo. Its speakers were blaring.

Earsplitting.

BLIP … BLIPBLIPBLIPBLIP …

The pitch from the device was painful, excruciating, and the bat creature was outraged by it. It halted and shrieked on the approach to the centre platform. The massive bat looked around, saw the other, stronger men stampeding towards it. The shouting men on the northwalk crossing over.

Jake tore off the power belt and grasped one end of it like it was a length of heavy chain. The creature had dragged Hanuma into deeper shadows. It was a murky shape now, with a single splash of light bouncing off its glistening, snouted head.

The bat thrust its wings violently forward as Jake swung the power belt in a high arc. Its weight of lead casings and batteries hit the creature on its skull. The bat let out a shriek, and its clawed legs flew out towards Jake. It snorted wildly, a stinking, vile mucus flying from its nostrils. Jake swung the belt again.

And again.

His father, with Dangari and Muras, was racing across the central platform. The bat had withdrawn its blood-covered fangs from Hanuma's neck and dropped him. The old man was still conscious, moaning on the walkway, as the bat turned. Suddenly, with a final shriek, the bat propelled itself over the side and plummeted toward the jungle floor.

Jake sunk to his knees and cradled Hanuma until the others reached him. Dangari and Muras helped tend to the wounded shaman. Dr Lefkovitz was riveted at the railing. He saw the falling monster spread its wings and go into a glide. It circled quickly, terrifyingly, then headed out towards the river and the jungle night.

It was a while before Jake and his father descended
in the sling. They waited below as Dangari and
Muras brought Hanuma down. Dr Lefkovitz
made the old man as comfortable as possible on
a cot of woven hemp in the main hut.

'You're going downstream to the missionary
village,' Dr Lefkovitz told the barely conscious
Hanuma. 'Jake told me what happened. We saw
the creature.'

'I'm sorry ... very sorry,' Hanuma said, gasping.
He struggled to hold his head up.

Jake got a pair of his jeans and a T-shirt.
He rolled them up and placed them under
Hanuma's head for a pillow. Dr Lefkovitz carefully
injected an anti-rabies vaccine into the folds of
Hanuma's stomach, and a local anaesthetic into
the periphery of the wounds at the back of his
neck. He cleaned and cauterized the punctures

and lacerations from the bite and attack. 'You'll need an intravenous drip to prevent you from going into shock. You save your energy – rest. Everything will be OK,' Dr Lefkovitz said gently.

Hanuma closed his eyes. He began to breathe deeply. His body was still trembling. Dangari draped Hanuma's old and frayed shaman robe about him to comfort him, to wrap him in the spirit and power and tribal dreams it still held for Hanuma.

'What'll happen at the missionary camp?' Jake asked.

'Their radio is powerful enough to reach the Brazilian Army installation at Jacaronda,' his father said. 'They'll send a medic in a helicopter and air-lift him to Manaus.'

METAMORPHOSIS

Magyar and three of the other men brought down the remains of the two dead workers. Dr Lefkovitz left the hut to examine what was left of the twisted and hollowed bodies. Jake stayed with Hanuma to make certain the drip needle didn't slip out of the wrist vein and bloat the arm. He himself was still shaken from the confrontation with the huge bat. He needed to talk alone with his father. It seemed to him there were a lot of questions that needed to be asked, and decisions to be made.

Sorgno, one of the younger workers, came in to check on Hanuma. Jake asked Sorgno to stay with the old man while he went out by the campfire and waited until he could get his father aside. Several of the other workers had already placed thick logs and chunks of peat on the campfires so they blazed, to help ward off the chill and the terror.

'Will Hanuma be all right?' Jake whispered to his father. 'The bite was deep. That thing's fangs were like knives. What kind of creature was it?'

'I've never seen or heard of any species of bat that large or ferocious,' his father said. 'Even in Indonesia the *megachiroptera* don't get half that big. The biggest bat known is a fruit bat.' His father's voice became strangely hollow, a tone Jake had long ago realized meant his father was filtering his words. Choosing too carefully what he wanted to say.

'You're not telling me something,' Jake said.

His father dropped his gaze to the ground. Jake knew that look, too – another familiar, evasive manoeuvre. 'Son, the Amazon is as big and unexplored as the depths of the ocean. There could be anything down here ...

'Dad, what don't you want me to know?'

Dr Lefkovitz turned to look at the roaring fires. 'We had a warning, I suppose. About the bat, perhaps. The first month the expedition had settled here, Hanuma and I took a pirogue and went upriver about a dozen miles to a small village – a malorca of Kano Indians – true primitives and known in past times to be headhunters. As we approached the village's mud beach, there were thirty or forty of the Kanos who had come down to the bank. Naked men with straw woven into their hair. Women with moonstone necklaces and holding children. Children played tag in the mud.'

'What happened?' Jake asked.

His father turned back to look Jake in the eye. 'Closer, I noticed several of the villagers throwing what looked like large chunks of meat and bone into the water. All around the "meat", the river boiled with the flash of silver fish. I insisted we stop. I asked Hanuma why the Kanos were feeding the piranha. Hanuma said we should keep going – that it would be dangerous to stop – but I wanted to know what was going on.

'Hanuma and I let the boat drift into the shallows, but we held our paddles ready. We had to circle around the massive school of feeding piranha, some of the fish were a foot – a foot and a half! – long. Larger than any piranha I'd ever seen. The fish hurled themselves at the food, sinking their teeth deep, then shaking their bodies ferociously until a shred of the meat tore loose. I saw what they were being fed: pieces of human bodies.'

Jake's tongue thickened. His shirt was damp, too tight about his chest.

His father went on. 'The villagers were tossing into the river parts of what seemed to have once been a man and a woman — perhaps a couple of children, too,' his father continued. 'Hands and feet that had been hacked off — the remains of a savage slaughtering.'

Jake fought the sickening feeling that was swelling in his stomach. 'Who killed them?'

'That's what I wanted to know. Hanuma called to the villagers. A shaman came forward and spoke in a language Hanuma understood. "The slaughtered men and women were a family," Hanuma translated for me. "The village had to kill them because the family was about to turn into beasts."'

'What was the shaman talking about?' Jake asked.

'Hanuma had another exchange, then tried to

explain to me that the shaman believed, in this village – every few years – some of them change into terrible winged creatures. Monsters that begin to kill and devour the other villagers. They hang their victims high in the jungle. Demons. Phantoms. The slaughtered family had begun its metamorphosis.'

'You and Hanuma didn't believe that, did you?' Jake asked.

'No,' his father said. '"*Get us out of here,*"' I told Hanuma. Together, we paddled back out, straight through the water boiling with the feeding piranha. Hanuma kept talking to the tribe's shaman. Smiling. Laughing. I knew Hanuma was calming the tribe. Assuring the shaman and villagers that we were leaving in peace ...'

'Do you think the winged monster could have been this big bat?' Jake asked. 'That this bat has been feeding on the village and they explained it with this metamorphosis – this crazy belief that people in the village could turn into monsters? I mean, that's nuts.'

'Yes,' his father said. 'But I should have listened more carefully. Asked more questions. I think they have seen this bat. Maybe there's more than one of them, but I don't think so. It's more likely that the giant we saw tonight is a single mutation. There are high levels of mercury in the water here from the gold mining upstream. Other chemicals from ore extractions and the logging. I think it's all connected, and if I'd heard the tribe out – if I didn't think they were so misguided, so unknowing and ignorant – perhaps I would know there was something real. A real terror. A truly monstrous creature that had mutated from the poisons. I sensed the danger. It was part of the reason I didn't want you to come down. There are many things in the jungle that don't have logical explanations. You have to go by feeling. The Indians can do that. They understand things I never could. They've had to keep instincts alive, instincts that are too buried in me to retrieve completely in one lifetime.'

'Maybe the bat's not a recent mutation,' Jake said. 'Maybe it's an evolved creature that has lived here all along – since time began – and it doesn't happen to like a lot of people invading its territory. You – the expedition – you're the real invaders around here, aren't you? I read a lot before deciding to come down here, Dad. The Indians have been here for twenty thousand years and everything went just fine. They took care of the jungle and the jungle took care of them.'

'That's got nothing to do with that bat . . .'

'It could,' Jake said. 'I mean, you couldn't blame the jungle if it started fighting back.' He remembered Hanuma. 'Hey, that bat could have given Hanuma rabies, right?'

'If it was infected, the virus would be in its spittle. In its bite.'

'Its saliva was in Hanuma's wounds,' Jake said. 'It was in his neck.'

'And upper spine,' his father added. 'If the bite was on Hanuma's hands or legs, he might have as much as three to six weeks before the symptoms of rabies – the madness – could begin. Once the virus reaches the brain, there's no cure. The rabies virus feeds on the brain cells and drives its victim insane. Hydrophobia. Fear of water. A horror of *everything* – in its final stages. It is the most terrifying death imaginable – but, even if Hanuma is infected, he's got a good chance of getting through this if we get him downstream tonight. I started his rabies shots, but he's going to require a series of them over several days. The Fathers at the village will continue the injections until the helicopter can get him to the hospital in Manaus.'

Dangari and Muras interrupted. They took Dr Lefkovitz aside, whispering for his ears only.

When he came back to Jake, his father said, 'They're ready to put Hanuma in the pirogue.'

'Dad, you've been here for months. You've got enough dead bats to choke a hippo. Besides, the whole place is going to flood any week now. How many more flying rats do you have to knock off?'

The sound of men chanting drifted to them from the edge of the camp. The workers were standing around the open grave they'd dug for the dead men. Dangari came over and asked Dr Lefkovitz to say a few words. Together they walked to the grave.

Muras made room for Jake to stand next to him as his father spoke in a prayerful tone:

'They were two loyal and fine friends – members of our research team. They were good family men and spoke often about their children. I will see that the monies they earned will reach their families. The museum sponsoring the expedition will provide extra funds. We

will do as much as we can . . .'

The grave was deep, moist, with sides that glistened in the moonlight. Jake lifted his eyes from the shadowy, twisted cadavers lying at the bottom of the grave, and glanced around the circle of men. He saw the worker he'd left with Hanuma.

If that guy's here, then who's with Hanuma? Jake thought with alarm. He counted heads. Everyone was standing around the grave except Hanuma. *Did you leave Hanuma alone?* Jake wanted to shout.

Jake turned as a cry shattered the night. Hanuma was standing in front of the blazing fire — the central fire roaring from extra logs and branches piled on to keep the creature away. The old man's hands clawed up toward the sky, as if he were trying to strangle a phantom. 'RANCA DI!' he screamed. 'GARA DI RANCA!'

Several of the men at the grave cried out as

Hanuma walked forward *into* the fire, wailing the words over and over.

'GARA DI RANCA!'

Dangari raced toward him. He and Muras reached him as the hem of his robe caught fire. He collapsed with a final scream.

The men tore the burning robe off of Hanuma. Magyar scooped water from the drinking trough and spilled it on Hanuma's legs. They laid him down and Dr Lefkovitz was at his side, kneeling, checking Hanuma's feet and ankles. His feet were calloused, black with charcoal. The other men surrounded them now, and Dr Lefkovitz heard the fear in their stammering.

'He isn't burned,' Dr Lefkovitz said, finally. 'A little singed hair on his legs, but he's fine.'

Dangari translated the English for those of the men who didn't understand.

'We should leave now for the village,' Muras said.

Dr Lefkovitz nodded.

Dangari and Muras covered Hanuma's naked body with a sheet and carried him to the beached pirogue they had prepared. They laid the old man down gently on a bed of crushed palm leaves and young ferns arranged in the dugout, and lifted the pirogue into the shallows. Muras took the bow seat, Dangari the stern. Workers waded into the pool and guided the pirogue until it was clear of the shallows. The rapid central flow of the river caught the dugout. Dangari and Muras grasped their paddles and began deep, rhythmic strokes into the dark water.

THE FALLS

Jake waved a solemn farewell with the others on the bank as the pirogue moved off swiftly downstream through the mist and moonlight. He asked his father, 'Did you give them a gun?'

'We have no guns,' his father said.

'You're kidding, right?'

'It's the law here, enforced by tribal decree. We are guests here for research. Spears. Traps. Poison darts and blow guns are used to slay animals for food. The Murdaruci can hit a parrot a hundred feet high in the trees. They often eat the parrots.'

Jake felt nauseous, but his own shivering had stopped. He was frightened about Hanuma's journey. He knew that the trip downstream to the missionary village wouldn't be long. He remembered the trip upstream very well, and estimated the pirogue would reach Dark Angel Falls in less than an hour.

'There are two other smaller falls between Dark Angel and the missionary camp,' his father said.

Jake recalled them and knew those wouldn't be a problem. What he worried about was how difficult it would be for Dangari and Muras to carry Hanuma and the dugout down the steep, rocky bank and past the violent whirlpools at the base of the tremendous drop of Dark Angel Falls.

The men returned to the grave. The sound of shovels thrusting into the dirt, and the thud as each scoop fell, was like the ticking of a clock.

Jake wanted to put his hands over his ears.

'What is "*Gara di ranca*"?' Jake asked Magyar. 'What was Hanuma saying?'

'It is Murdaruci,' Magyar said. 'Hanuma was furious at the sky and the Great Spirit. He had fever. A sickness in his head. I'm certain that he didn't know what he was saying. It was a question.'

'What?'

'Hanuma asked the Great Spirit why it had sent us doom.'

Dangari worried as the mist of the river became as blinding as fog. He and Muras paddled quietly, doing nothing to mute or sully the sounds of the rushing water. They knew the pure sounds of the river, and, if they listened carefully, they could navigate a pirogue on it blindfolded. They would hear the white water and falls in plenty of time to find a favourite safe pool or backwater near the bank.

There was a break in the mist and they saw a flight of pink ibis fly across the front of the bow and up into the moonlight. White-collared marabou storks strutted along a marshy bank. Muras caught a glimpse of a jaguar sitting high in a rubber tree.

Soon, the blinding mist returned and closed down upon them like a white ceiling. Dangari leaned forward and placed a cool hand on Hanuma's brow. The old, thin shaman looked like he was sleeping. His waist-long hair fanned out at his sides and stirred in the river wind.

'We'll soon be at the village,' Dangari whispered in Murdaruci. Soothing. Wanting the old man to know he was with his good and trusted friends. His favourite workers . . .

Hanuma's eyes opened. He moved his lips, but no words could be heard.

'You rest,' Muras said. 'The Fathers will

be happy to see you.'

Hanuma smiled. He listened to the sound of wavelets slapping at the hull. The pirogue rocked gently with each plunge of a paddle. He stared up at the billowing whiteness above him, felt as if he could reach up his hand and touch it like a ceiling. He heard the sounds of the ibis and jumping fish. The movement of a large alligator across the muddy bank. Hanuma wanted to believe the journey would go well. He heard the rush of the water against the rocks. Without raising his head, he knew exactly where they were on the river.

'We will be at Dark Angel soon,' Dangari said.

Hanuma nodded. He thought about sleeping until then. He turned his head to the side and smelled the freshness of the palm and fern bedding beneath him. He wouldn't think about the bat. The creature. He was too weak for that. He decided to believe he was in a swing. Yes, that was it. The dugout was a hammock – like his father had once made for him out of twisted vines and the bark of a kapok tree.

But there came another sound.

Dangari heard it first. His hearing was always the best. At first, he believed it was a large stork or night heron taking flight upstream. It was a flapping of wings. Large wings. Something large flying toward them.

The flapping noise grew louder. Whatever it was, it was just above them now. Something flying, hidden by the mist.

Something following them.

EFFIGIES

Jake knew Hanuma's outburst had terrorized the workers. From time to time, he had seen frightened people at accident scenes in Manhattan. Firemen as they arrived at a tenement that was a flaming inferno. Victims strewn on the sidewalk of Fifth Avenue after a bus jumped the curve and ploughed into a crowd of Christmas shoppers. Frightened men and women had a look in their eyes from the smell of fear. Time seemed to stand still, and sometimes they babbled nearly incoherently. They walked in circles and blessed themselves and wept.

The Indians tonight moved quickly to set several more camp fires about the grounds and shouted at the night to try to keep the monstrous creature away. The fires blazed, fueled by the logs and kindling that had been intended to last at least three more weeks or until the floods hit.

Dr Lefkovitz didn't try to stop the men from their fire-building. He knew it was what any jungle village would do if a man-eater was on the prowl. The jaguars and pumas would occasionally grab a small child from play and race off with it into the jungle. Rarely did a large cat brazenly invade a camp and attack a man or woman, even at night.

With Dangari and Muras transporting Hanuma downstream, there was only Magyar with enough English to communicate clearly what was happening. Several of the men had taken hammers and what remained of the two-by-fours brought up from Manaus. Others tore apart a lean-to and begun to make a dozen or so of what appeared to be large crosses.

'What are they doing?' Jake asked his father.

'Making effigies,' his father said.

The workers began to gather bundles of yellow reeds and young bamboo from the bank, and tie them on to the wooden structures so they appeared to have arms and legs and heads. The figures took shape and, when held upright, stood five and six feet tall.

'It's really weird,' Jake said. 'Shouldn't they be doing something else?'

'It'd be like telling Kansas farmers they can't have scarecrows,' his father said. 'They think the effigies will fool the bat like they can trick a jaguar. I've seen tribes do it in India and Africa, too. Scarecrows to fool man-eaters – rogue lions and tigers – that there are many more warriors than there really are. In the South Indian swamps, the families make effigies and wear masks on the back of their heads.'

'Why the *back* of their heads?'

'Most big cats don't attack from the front. They don't attack if you're looking at them. The masks on the back of the natives' heads are a trick that works for a while, but sometimes the animals catch on. They get so they can tell – perhaps smell! – which are the real faces and real people. Then the masks don't work any more.'

The workers used hammers and an axe handle to drive the base of the life-size effigies into the soft ground. Jake found the sight of the scarecrows standing around the camp really scary. 'Why don't we just get out of here?' Jake said.

'There are some very important things I need to do before I can leave,' his father said. 'I can arrange for a couple of the workers to take you downstream in the morning. These men aren't experienced enough to be on the river at night.'

'What are you talking about?' Jake said. 'I'm not leaving without you. My blood's the same as yours, Pops. Sure, you're smarter, but I'm more of an athlete. And I've got Gizmo. You've got to see what Gizmo can do.'

For a moment, Jake thought his father could see how he'd changed. 'I could use every man,' his father said, finally, 'but it's best if you go.'

'Hey, you *need* me.'

His father dropped his gaze. 'We'll talk about this later. Now I need to talk to the men. It'd be better if you wait in the hut. The men would feel strange with you there.'

'Oh, yeah,' Jake said. 'I forgot I'm not a member of the team.'

Jake spun on his heel and marched himself into the hut, slapping closed its canvas door-flap so it made a *whaaack*. He heard his father calling Magyar to gather the men around the central campfire. Jake threw himself down on his cot, and clasped his hands around the back of his neck. He stared at the yellowing, thatched ceiling. *Why does the bat eat brains?* he wondered. Sure, there are other animals that go straight for the organs and marrow of their prey. What kind of creature feasts on the human mind?

Dangari was thankful the sound of the wings had gone away. There had been something above them for a few minutes – something hidden in the thick night fog, and then had moved on.

'We should start to head for shore,' Dangari said to Muras.

'Yes,' Muras said.

The river was narrowing before the falls, and the flow was faster. Dangari was thankful when they passed around a final turn and there was a break in the mist and river fog. Moonlight lit the way clear to the falls. There was ample time to rudder the boat toward the largest backwater pool on the left bank. It was when they guided the boat towards the haven that they saw a dark shape hanging from the gnarled trunk of a grandiflora tree.

Dangari tried not to sound frightened. 'We must head for the other shore.'

'Yes,' Muras agreed.

Hanuma stirred from his sleep. He had somehow heard a fear creep into his friends' voices. He began to send his thoughts skyward to ask the Great Spirit to protect them. *Get us to the village safely*, Hanuma prayed. *If I have ever been a kind and good shaman, let us pass the Dark Angel ... let us pass ...*

His body started to tremble again. He tried to raise his head, but he was too weak.

Dangari and Muras turned the boat. The falls were still far enough away for them to make it to the right bank of thick, lush jungle. Even without a backwater pool or cover, they could grasp the dense overhang of mogno branches and berry vines, and stop the boat.

The bat waited until the pirogue was in the middle of the river before it dropped away from the tree trunk and took to the air. Dangari saw it gliding toward them, its shining, immense wings strangely beautiful in the moonlight.

'Faster,' Dangari told Muras.

Muras dug his paddle harder and deeper into the water. The current was treacherous now. It would take all their strength to reach the bank before the eddies and white water would totally seize the boat.

Dangari needed to keep his focus on plunging his paddle with more power. Deeper still. He couldn't think about the flapping sound. The sound of the wings behind him came closer. He felt a shadow pass between him and the moon.

Muras, too, cut his paddle into the water with more strength and speed than he'd thought possible. Panic began to creep into his stomach, and a stench of rotting carrion descended and burned in his nostrils. The fluttering of wings became drowned out by the roar of the falls. Dangari leaned forward as he stabbed the water with his paddle. There was still a chance, he thought. As long as the creature didn't attack. As long as they could keep the boat lunging forward toward the land.

Rudder the boat and make it to the overhang.

They could be safe.

Abruptly, the blackness swooped down. That was all Dangari could see at first: a huge, rippling blackness in front of him. He felt the pirogue shudder and rock as the dark thing struck the boat. Muras was immediately spilled into the turbulent water. There was no time for words.

No cries for help. Muras tried to swim out of the current which took hold of him with the force of a whirlpool.

Dangari struck fiercely at the water with his paddle. Alone, he changed his stroke, driving his paddle deep, then turning it outward to maintain a shred of rudder control. For a few moments longer, he wanted to believe there would be an escape.

Suddenly – frighteningly – Hanuma's body began to rise in the boat. At first, Dangari thought the old man was helping to ward off the bat.

It looked like he was *standing*.

Finally, Dangari understood. The bat, its wings fluttering wildly, had grasped Hanuma by his throat. It held him high, biting violently at Hanuma's neck, holding him aloft like a rag doll.

There came a scream from ahead, and Dangari glimpsed Muras being washed over the falls.

Dangari swung his paddle at the bat. He tried to stand and tear the creature's glistening wings, but he was thrown off balance and the dugout capsized.

The bed of palm leaves and ferns boiled about Dangari like confetti and the current seized him. As the river hurled him towards the great drop, he saw a moss-covered rock near the edge. For a second, hope swelled in him, but he was swept past the rock. He saw the overturned pirogue and tried to grab on to it. Perhaps it would become wedged between rocks or sunken branches or ...

He couldn't hold on.

Preparing to die, Dangari saw what looked like a clump of weeds floating in the current with him. His hands grasped at the long flowing white strands. For an instant they felt like a heavenly silkiness. They made him think of an angel's hair. Delicate hair. Flowing. An angel had come for him. That was his final thought before he glimpsed the open dark mouth and the glint of a gold tooth in the moonlight.

For a moment, the current buoyed him. As he washed over the brink of the falls, he realized he was clutching Hanuma's severed head.

SOUNDS

Dr Lefkovitz took the first two-hour shift as lookout, feeding the campfires in case the bat decided to come back. The terror of the night and jet lag had socked into Jake. Finally, he fell into a deep sleep.

Several of the younger men worked on their life-size effigies long into the night, until the silhouettes and mud faces looked eerily real in the flickering firelight. Two of the strongest workers took the second shift, and Magyar asked to handle the watch closest to dawn – when he'd have to be up anyway, preparing food for the men.

Magyar waited until everyone was asleep before he decided to scout the perimeter of the camp. He found the morning shift more of an inconvenience than anything frightening. He hadn't seen the bat himself, and in truth, he was used to the exaggerations of his tribesmen. They were always coming to him with tales of a ten-foot carp they'd seen in the river, or an alligator as long as a tree. Magyar knew, as a rule, to cut in half the size of any animal or lizard or fish anyone ever claimed to see anywhere.

He'd seen the bodies of the two men, but small bats, ocelots, or a jaguar could have inflicted the same mutilations. He knew there was a large bat that had been blamed, but he'd seen as few as a handful of rodents and large beetles devour half a dead human within a day or so. They, too, went for the eyes with its entrances to soft, moist flesh. Carcasses of any sort never lasted long in the jungle.

What Magyar was concerned about was sorts of meats he could supply in the two weeks remaining before the expedition was to head back to Manaus. As he scouted close to the edge of the jungle, there were sounds of small animals and, perhaps, night herons scurrying about in the undergrowth. He knew the men would be happy if he could make a fresh kill. A roast tapir or a few large white monkeys would pick everyone's spirits up. He could hear the praise he'd get if he could serve something freshly caught.

One deep rustling caught Magyar's attention where the jungle thickened into a hammock of mangrove trees at the river's edge. There, amidst the vines and branches, he'd harvested several large snakes and turtle eggs over the last few weeks. He took a hunting dart from his chest sling, slid it into his blowpipe, and headed into the shadows.

He heard the rustling again.

Magyar could feel his mouth go dry and his pulse begin to quicken. The hunt always excited him, and he was certain he'd outsmart whatever was hiding in the maze and darkness of the mangrove roots. He could already smell the fresh animal flesh cooking on a spit turning over the fire. He knew he'd use the drippings of a fresh monkey or parrot to mix with flour into a blood paste, a delicacy among his tribesmen. He knew a good blood paste would boost everyone's morale, and they would forget about the silly bat.

As a head cook and hunter for many years, his eyesight in darkness was as keen as a river hawk. He took a few steps, then halted and listened. Another step. And another, and then stopped again.

The rustle. The animal breathing. It was still there.

Magyar prided himself on being able to stalk closer to any prey than all of the hunters of his tribe. He wouldn't be a fool. He didn't want to get too far from the light of the fires and the protecting effigies. The rustlings he heard were different than others he'd known. It seemed to be something large. Something crawling. He began to pray for a very large and fat iguana or gecko. He stopped when he saw a dark shape just ahead of him.

A boar, he thought.

He would roast another boar...

Suddenly, the dark shape was moving fast toward him. He was shocked by its swiftness, something reaching him and whisking up from the blackness at his feet. A thought, the Murdaruci equivalent of *What is it?* shot through Magyar's mind. Whatever the thing was, it rushed up his body knocking the blowpipe from his lips. It had the weight of a large animal, and he opened his mouth to cry out.

To shout . . .

But there was no sound.

No terrible pain.

Only a great pressure at his throat and a cracking of bone and cartilage. A moment later and he could feel a vice of needle teeth that rendered his jaw frozen. He was on the ground now – on his back – and whatever it was held him down with the force and precision of a puma. Like a jungle cat, it had him by the neck, this thing, this black thing that now began to flap its wings on either side of him.

It took Magyar a moment to realize that the creature that held him was convulsing, the whole of its body shaking, vomiting fluids directly into his throat and mouth and . . .

Magyar gasped. By now he knew everything

Dr Lefkovitz and Jake and the other workers had said was true. A patch of the night fog had broken straight up to the canopy. Moonlight crashed down through the hammock, and he could see a part of the bat's head. Grotesquely shaped, wet membranes unfurled from its nostrils and ears. Dr Lefkovitz had taught him the anatomy of bats. Magyar gazed curiously into the large, intense and black eyes.

A moment more, and he knew whatever the fluids were that the creature was pumping into his throat were drugging him – clouding his mind. They were numbing, dulling all pain now. He was paralyzed.

The bat relaxed and disengaged its teeth from his neck. It crawled off of him and circled him for a moment. When its full face hovered over him once more, it was staring at him sideways. A long, narrow tongue slid out from between its needle teeth and began to lick Magyar's eyelids.

Magyar felt the moist touch of the tongue.

It was gentle. Cooling.

Absurdly, Magyar felt hope flowing back into his thoughts. He knew if the saliva was like the small vampires', it would slowly dissolve the skin from his face. It would make his cheeks bleed, and the bat would take its time savouring the blood.

It would lick carefully.

With delight.

Slowly.

Like he'd seen the smaller bats do with their prey in the canopy.

There would be time, Magyar believed. Time for someone to awaken and realize he was missing from his watch. Dr Lefkovitz, or one of the men, would look out to the fire and effigies, and realize something was wrong. They'd track him the short distance he'd travelled into the jungle. They would find him. The bat would hear them coming and it would fly off and away from him.

Suddenly, he saw the bat's mouth like a constrictor's. The full spectrum of its horrible teeth and crimson-coated gums floated over him now, dripping with what he knew now was his own blood.

No, he thought. Oh, God ...

With a quick burst of saliva, two small openings in the creature's upper gums undulated, and a pair of hollow, sharp fangs began to emerge. They slid downward – seven, eight inches! – and locked into place with the precision of dental drills. Convulsing again, the bat lowered the fangs until they entered Magyar's eyes. Moments later, still conscious – even in blindness – Magyar knew the bat was drinking his mind.

Dr Lefkovitz awakened as the first light of dawn touched the camp. He went outside expecting to see Magyar cooking breakfast meats and stirring a steaming pot of boiling roots mixed with the dried mushrooms and fish that had been brought up from Manaus. The effigies stood in the morning mist.

'Magyar,' Dr Lefkovitz called softly, near the central fire. All the fires had burned low, but he thought it was just Magyar conserving the logs as dawn had approached. When there was no answer, Dr Lefkovitz became concerned.

A wind came up from the mountains, and cleared the view to the river. Dr Lefkovitz decided he'd look for Magyar on the bank. He was always catching fresh river bass and frogs to blend into his soups and pastes. The sun hadn't dried the mud bank, and it was easy to spot the fresh footprints. Dr Lefkovitz knew about the riches of the mangrove hammock.

'Hey,' he called out again. 'Magyar!'

The mangrove roots rose high above the jungle floor. Several crawling sucker-fish had left the water and climbed into the roots to feed on moths and stick bugs. Dr Lefkovitz found his sandals sinking into a squishing mud. He was several feet from the bank now, and was afraid the river had begun to rise and swell the watershed and pockets of quicksand – the first sign that the annual flood was imminent.

There was an odour of decay in the air, and it began to sting Dr Lefkovitz's nostrils. He tried to shake off his sleep, and as he prised his foot loose from the mud, he looked down and noticed the mud had an unusual red tint to it. He stepped back away from it, and felt something cracking beneath his feet. It looked like a white branch. But there were other sprigs of white and—

He realized he was looking at pieces of a skull.

At first he thought they were from some animal, but then he saw a rib cage. It looked human – but barely – and it was only the shape of the jawbone that gave it away. Dr Lefkovitz began to call out, to shout, as he realized he was standing in the middle of something very bad. The flecks of bone and flesh sprayed across the mud like confetti. He saw now that the whole jungle floor was moving, alive with beetles carrying tiny pieces of human flesh to their lairs in the earth and roots beneath fallen trees.

Even as he shouted to awaken the whole camp, he knew what had happened to Magyar. He understood that – and what would have to be done.

THE TRAP

A half dozen workers were stringing garlands of leaves and shredded bamboo over the netting, pulleys, and support ropes, camouflaging the reality that the new addition to the riverwalk was, in truth, a trap.

'Tighter,' Dr Lefkovitz was shouting to Rasdyr, the smallest of the workers, who could climb to the very top of the canopy's thinnest branches. 'Pull the ropes tighter.'

Rasdyr, his body already dripping in the hot

morning sun, smiled broadly and signalled that he understood.

'How does it work?' Jake asked his father when he came up in the sling. 'It looks like some kind of jerry-rigged batting cage.'

'It's basically a room made of very strong rope and jungle vines,' his father said. 'When that monster returns, it will have to land at the end of the riverwalk and crawl forward.' Jake followed his father inside the rope chamber. 'One end of the trap will be left open.'

'How do you know it'll come in?' Jake asked.

'There will be something it wants inside.'

'What?'

'Bait.'

'What kind?'

'Human.'

Jake glared at his father. 'Dad, didn't that thing kill enough people? Who's going to be nuts enough to be in here?'

'I'll be in the trap,' his father said. 'Me and Rasdyr.' He pointed to the opening. 'When the bat crawls in, it'll trip a rope trigger that'll fly two additional nets into place – sealing the trap and dividing the chamber. We'll be safe in this half. The bat will be trapped in the other half. We can fire darts into it until it falls unconscious.'

'*Unconscious*?'

'Yes,' his father said, stripping his voice of any emotion. 'I want to capture it alive.'

Jake knew his father was fighting to contain a swell of fear and hate and vengeance. 'Why alive?' he asked.

'Jake, you've got to realize what all this might mean for the expedition,' his father said. 'For the museum. We could study the creature. Use it. Learn from it. We have no idea what its biology and behavior can tell us. How does its brain work? What is its chemistry?'

'It ate the brains out of a few of your men,'

Jake said. 'Didn't that tell you enough? At least it's a hint!'

'We could know more ...'

'Dad, you're not a trapper or hunter!'

'I used net traps in Indonesia long before you were born, son,' his father said. 'I developed them for a British zoological project to save the orang-utans in the Javanese jungles. An adult male orang-utan has the strength of two or three men – they are ferociously strong. You corner a primate like that and it's capable of ripping the arms off of you. These net traps worked just fine. We saved over forty – fifty! – orang-utans by catching them and relocating them deeper into the jungle and out of the reach of poachers.'

'Dad, there's still time for us to leave. Don't you really think that's what we should do?' Jake asked. 'We could load the pirogues and be out of here before the night ...'

His father didn't answer him. He took Jake

down in the sling to the jungle floor. Two of the workers were loading a single pirogue with fresh supplies. 'I want you to leave,' his father said.

'I'm not going with them,' Jake said.

His father took him into the main hut. He pointed to Jake's belongings on the floor next to his cot. 'You've got to pack. Your coming here was a mistake, son. I knew there was danger ...'

Jake felt like yelling at his father: OH, YOU'RE NOT BLAMING THIS ONE ON ME. NOT THIS SUCKER   YOU'RE NOT GOING TO TURN THIS INTO ONE MORE BIG GUILT TRIP FOR ME – but he knew that wouldn't get him anywhere. 'Is all of this your ego, Dad?' he said. 'Just so everyone back at the museum might say, "Oh, boy, Lefkovitz caught a big bat." Why do you care so much about bats? About this bat! This bat belongs here. Oh, it's a homicidal monster all right, but this is its home. All those specimens you've got in those jars. It's like you're trying to be a control freak with nature. You want to be bigger than God.'

'No, I'm not trying to play God,' his father objected.

'Well, a lot of you scientists are,' Jake said. 'Your pals at the museum. At the labs. A lot of them are cloning. Splitting genes. Don't you think a lot of it is a bit creepy? You can just imagine what they'd do with this bat.'

'No ...'

'I think you do.'

'Son, when I decided to become a scientist — that meant I had to follow the research frontier wherever it took me. You'd probably be dead now from polio or smallpox or some other disease if it wasn't for exploration and daring and discovery. I and millions of people would be dead without vaccines and medical treatments. We've always lived on one cutting edge or another. That's what a scientist does. That's what I do. Just because

I'm here in the Amazon, it's no different. There will be things we'll learn from this bat. From its behaviour and chemistry and genes. We have a chance here, Jake ...'

'A chance for what?'

'I don't expect you to understand.'

'You can't go around doing whatever you want, Dad. It's all gone too far. What will you or some experimenting whacko do with this monster's genes? Clone big bats? Splice its genetic material into genes of corn to grow bigger crops? They've put fish genes into tomatoes. Mixed spider genes with goats – so that now they've created goats that have strands of webbing in their milk. They've already cloned barnyard animals so there are sheep born with two heads and five legs. It's nuts. Enough! It's wrong. It's too fast. They can't get our orders straight at a drive-in hamburger joint. Pops, don't mess with this bat. Leave it alone and let's get out of here!'

Exhausted, Jake's father sat on the edge of his cot. For a few moments he stared at Jake, then moved his gaze to the stack of specimen jars, a ray of sunlight cutting through them so the faces of the creatures appeared cruel and macabre. For the first time in his life, Jake's father had no quick dismissal for him. 'I think you'd better show me your Gizmo,' his father said, quietly. 'I'd like to see what it is.'

A small smile crept on to Jake's face. 'Sure, Dad,' he said. 'Sure.'

'I know it translates sound reflections into images,' his father said.

Jake moved quickly and turned Gizmo on. 'It does a lot more than that.' Its narrow rectangular screen glowed. He attached a wide headband to the ends of the screen, and placed the lit screen against his forehead. 'The images that appear on the screen can be sensed on my brow,' Jake said. 'On anyone's forehead ...'

'What are you talking about?'

'The images have different heat patterns and so I can "see" without using my eyes. I can tell the rough shape of objects in total darkness, even with my eyes closed.'

'We can do that with infra-red binoculars . . .'

'Yeah,' Jake said. 'But you don't have any military power infra-red anything on this expedition. All you've got in that department is me and Gizmo. If you're going to be hunting any giant, brain-eating bat, then I have to be with you in that trap. You need to know when it's coming for you. You need to know where it is in the trap, even in pitch black.'

Dr Lefkovitz reached out and took the screen and headband from his son. He placed the glowing screen so it was flat against his own forehead.

'I can't feel or see anything. There's a little heat. No images. Son, this isn't the time for hocus-pocus.'

'I'm the only one here that's trained to be able to "see" with this thing. It takes practice. Weeks – months! – of practice like I had preparing for the science fair. Dad, that bat knew exactly which electrical wires and lighting systems to knock out on the riverwalk. It's very, very smart. It eats human brains. Who knows what that can really do? Who knows what happens if a creature eats nothing but brain proteins, amino acids and nuclei and ...? I mean, who *really* knows?

'Pops,' Jake continued, 'half of the Darwinian stuff in evolution is already up for grabs. There are all kinds of theories. All I know is that being able to see by means of sound and heat pictures on your forehead is not nuts. It's already scientific *fact*. They're using devices like Gizmo with blind people. That's where I got the idea. There are articles on it in the recent science extracts. You've just been too busy with all your bats down here to keep up with new stuff. Dad, Gizmo works – and if you're going to be the human bait in that trap, then I've got to be in there with you. I'm the only one trained on Gizmo – and you need me as part of the team. You really need me!'

Suddenly, there were cries and shouts from outside the hut. Jake and his father rushed outside. Several of the workers had hurried to meet a man staggering out of the jungle toward them. It was a moment before Jake and his father realized it was Muras, covered with mud and blood.

'IT FOLLOWED US ...' Muras was screaming. He saw Dr Lefkovitz and started toward him. The men put their arms around Muras and helped him the final distance.

'IT KILLED HANUMA. THE THING, THE BIG BAT KILLED HIM AND DANGARI ... IT FOLLOWED US ... IT FOLLOWED OUR PIROGUE ...'

Muras collapsed in Dr Lefkovitz's arms.

Jake ran and got his father's medicine kit. Rasdyr brought water from the trough. As Dr Lefkovitz cleaned the scrapes and cuts on Muras, the workers began to panic and weep. Several shouted angrily at the sky and the jungle and the failed effigies. They cried out with rage and grief.

'Now I've got to stay,' Jake told his father. 'The bat isn't going to let anyone leave. You know that now, don't you, Dad? *Don't you?*'

'Yes,' his father said. 'I know it.'

WAITING ...

*B*y nightfall Rasdyr, Jake and his father had settled in at the back of the trap. The three of them remained silent for a long while. Jake knew that each of them was thinking of Magyar and Hanuma – Dangari and the workers in their graves.

Rasdyr was barely five feet tall and, at twenty-eight, he still looked more like a boy than a man. His slight build reminded Jake of the jockeys he'd seen on the occasions when his father had taken him along with him and a few of his colleagues for a day at Yonkers trotter racetrack.

The Indian sat in the middle of the riverwalk platform, which formed the floor of the bat trap. He had separated his darts into two separate, small piles. One set of darts had been dipped in a drugging mixture distilled from the sap of wildflowers and eucalyptus trees. The others were coated with a mixture concentrated from oleander roots, a poison capable of slaying the largest of tapirs and wild boar.

'Check and recheck everything,' Dr Lefkovitz said. 'When the bat comes, we won't have much time.'

Jake held back tears as he checked and rechecked the battery belt and wire connections that powered Gizmo. He was remembering gentle little Hanuma, with his long grey hair and the gold tooth, waiting for him at the airport in Manaus. Jake had respected the no-nonsense approach Hanuma had taken with him. Throughout all their banter, travelling in the taxi and upriver, there had always been a wisdom and great sweetness in Hanuma's eyes and words.

Why did the bat have to stalk you? he thought silently to Hanuma. *Did it know you were the leader of the men? The shaman and commander of the Indian workers who had invaded its territory? Has it been watching? Its brain knowing – calculating! – more than we could ever know? It didn't attack you for food. Maybe revenge – for you betraying the pact your ancestors had with the jungle. Did the bat doom you because you helped lead Dad's expedition here?*

That was often the way Jake was able to deal with someone that had died – send his thoughts and terrors and fears to him or her. He had had a grandmother that was very much like Hanuma. Smart. Religious. When Grandma Jenna had fallen down and broken her hip, he had gone to the hospital every day to visit her. He had watched helplessly as the old woman had drifted into pneumonia. He held his grandmother in her final hour as she gasped for air.

'Don't be afraid of death,' she had whispered to him even then. They were her last words. 'Don't be afraid.'

'Dad, why do you think the bat is killing?' Jake asked softly.

'I don't know,' his father said, not turning his gaze from the shadows at the entrance to the trap. 'Sometimes I think of it as having watched me from the beginning. That it was always up there somewhere in the night as we harvested our specimens. The day Hanuma and I came back from the Kanos village – from the slaughtering – it was nearly dusk. We were still on the river and in a heavy fog and mist. There was the sound of something in the sky above us. Something large and unseen. We thought it might have been a stork or a condor lost from the mountains. Now I think the bat may have singled out Hanuma and me — that we were being tracked.'

'The night it attacked Hanuma,' Jake said, 'it passed me by. It could have got to me first. It would have been easier to kill me, but it didn't.'

'I've thought about that. I think the bat wanted Hanuma. That it sensed we're the leaders. Hanuma and I. It wanted to get rid of us. Now there's only me.'

Waiting in the trap, Jake was a mixture of fear and vengeance. He felt a deep wrath stirring inside of him, and it shocked him. His hatred went beyond any concern for his own safety. Jake had seen the remains of Magyar, and now following the news of Hanuma he could only think of the bat as being profoundly evil. He loved animals — but this was something more. It was a mistake by Nature. It was an unforgivable aberration.

'I want us to settle the score,' Jake said slowly. Bitterly. 'I want us to get even.'

Rasdyr and his father nodded. One look into Jake's eyes and they knew what anguish he was feeling.

Dr Lefkovitz had given strict instructions for the men at the camp to keep the fires burning high and to cluster together until the night was over.

'It's like we're in a trap within a trap,' Jake said. 'That bat isn't going to be happy until it kills us all. We're already trapped at the camp.'

'I think we are,' Dr Lefkovitz said.

'Everyone else seems to know it's not going to stop until it kills all of us,' Jake said. 'That's the only reason why no one's taking off into the jungle, no less leaving on the river in one of the dugouts. They already know what will happen if they try that.'

For a while, Dr Lefkovitz kept a Coleman lamp

lit at the centre of the trap. He and Rasdyr checked all the knots and pulleys. Jake kept Gizmo trained toward the opening and riverwalk where the bat could enter.

'What if the trip rope doesn't work?' Jake asked. 'That thing wouldn't think twice about charging all three of us.'

'It'll work,' Dr Lefkovitz said.

Something moved in the blackness of the riverwalk where the platform stretched out above the river, and the light from the Coleman paled.

'Monkeys,' Rasdyr said.

Jake nodded. He could see the shapes on Gizmo. They were small ones – several of them. Marmosets, perhaps, or a family of woollys.

Dr Lefkovitz held a machete ready. For the first time, Jake saw that his father was deeply anxious and frightened. Rasdyr slid one of the drug-tipped darts into a blowpipe. He had already loaded several of the reserve pipes and had laid them out neatly in front of him, like a surgeon's tools. Faint vapours from the sap had risen and mixed with the sweat on his face. He scratched with his long fingernails at the irritation he felt on his cheeks and forehead.

By three in the morning, Rasdyr appeared tired and needful of a nap. He had worked hard all day preparing the darts and carving the blowpipes. Occasionally a strong wind would blow off the river and the fires and lean-tos of the camp could be glimpsed far beneath them.

'Who taught you how to hunt?' Jake asked Rasdyr.

'My father taught me how to stay alive in the jungle.' Rasdyr tried to smile, but it turned into a yawn. He took water from a canteen and slapped it on his face. 'He knew many skills.'

Soon, the night mist had blown off the canopy and the river, and they could see the moon directly above them. The treetops were aglow, silver and shimmering. Dr Lefkovitz turned off the Coleman, and the three waited in silence again. They could hear the gurgling sounds of the river and see it sparkle like a thick glittering ribbon below and south of the walkway.

Dr Lefkovitz moved slowly closer to the centre of the trap. He listened to every peep and chirp and gentle crackling of the canopy.

There was a loud whooshing somewhere ahead, and Jake felt a chill crawl up his neck and across his scalp. There were new smells in the canopy now: dust, and a jasmine fragrance in the air. The late hour and crisp moonlight began to play tricks with his eyes and blur his vision. His mind was racing. All the death and loss that had happened was beginning to shift and seep into places in his brain and heart, where he couldn't escape it.

Jake realized the three of them were waiting like cheese in a mousetrap. He sat left of Rasdyr on a bed of leaves camouflaging the walkway. Panic swelled in him until he felt as if he were in a speeding car about to crash. There was the scream of a river loon – and his stomach hardened into a knot.

Suddenly, the chattering and whir of monkeys and insects disappeared. An utter stillness fell on the canopy, so that the only sound was the faint march of the river as it washed against the banks and churned downstream into white water.

More silence.

Dr Lefkovitz had heard a silence like this before when he had been in Java, and in the lush mountains of Kenya. It was a silence that preceded the arrival of the king of a vast primate colony. That's how it had been with the monkeys and apes: first, a shrieking that froze one's heart, and then an utter, uncanny silence while all the lesser monkeys awaited the appearance of the royal apes in the pecking order.

A breeze crept into the canopy. Jake saw an image fluttering at the centre of Gizmo's screen.

'Dad, it's coming.'

His father moved closer to watch the ghostly electronic picture. The night mist had conjured itself once more, thick enough to blacken out the moonlight. Now the men heard something in the sky.

A thing soaring overhead.

A few moments later, they heard it again. The glide of a large, airborne creature closing in.

There were vibrations now. The platform shaking. The creature had landed on the platform ahead of them. For a moment, the vague image disappeared from the screen and there were new sounds behind them. Then to the left and right.

Jake shifted, and redirected Gizmo. It was when he turned to check the trap's opening, that he noticed the shadow – as if a large tree branch were moving in a breeze. Rasdyr coughed. A moment later, the stench reached Jake's nostrils. His father had already covered his mouth. It was the horrid smell of rotting meat, like chicken that had stayed weeks too long in its package.

There came a wheezing sound, and the shadow crawled forward.

ENCOUNTER

A sliver of moonlight broke through again. Now Jake could see the reflection in the pair of huge glass eyes that stared at him. He saw the wet, dripping snout of the huge chiroptera lifted up into the night breeze. It sniffed fiercely.

Intensely.

Catching the full lure of the scent of human flesh, the shadow continued forward. The boards of the platform creaked beneath its weight. Bunched up, it appeared to be the size of a small car. As one of its wings lifted from its body, Jake thought the bat had surely passed the trip rope – the waiting trigger of jungle vine and fishing catgut and rope. One wing moved so that it protruded to the left. The bat crawled closer still.

'It should be *now*,' Rasdyr whispered.

The bat stopped.

Jake's eyes had become accustomed to the night and darkness and the shadows of the moonlight. He could see the bat swivelling its head as if sensing something wrong. Dangerous. It lifted its head and sniffed again toward the three figures crouched at the far end of the vine cluster. It decided to proceed. As it did, its talons dragged across the trip rope.

There was the quick pivoting of rope and pulleys, a dropping of log weights on either side of the net which made the inner mesh rise in a scream. Guide wires screeched, and the bat shuddered with surprise. The netting at the centre of the room was in place now, and the entrance behind the bat was sealed. The bat was caught inside the rope cage.

As the final counterweights pulled taut the top of the trap, the bat sat midway between the platform railings. It watched the physics of the entrapment, swivelling its head from left to right. When all the sounds had halted, it gazed toward the net roof with what looked more like curiosity than fear.

Jake and Rasdyr were startled that the trap had worked. They stared through the net divider at the freakish creature looking back at them. They could see that the bat's eyes and its every instinct had focused on them.

There was a snorting that deepened into a wheezing. Its jaws opened, and a hot froth dripped from the bat's lips.

Jake gasped. He could see the bat more

objectively now than in the madness of the first night when it had attacked Hanuma. It seemed to be staring at Gizmo in his hands and then lifted its lazy gaze and fixed its eyes on him. Jake's pulse quickened, as he believed the bat remembered him.

The bat twisted its head to the right, keeping one dark, terrible eye on Gizmo and Jake. The reek of its mouth announced the mark of the carnivore, and its wheezing transmuted into a hissing sound like a massive cobra. It moved forward, its taloned feet dragging along the planking like those of a gargoyle come to life on the edge of an ancient rampart.

It turned one ear in the direction of Gizmo.

Instinctively, Jake moved nearer to his father, who held a machete ready. Dr Lefkovitz took the full measure of the maze of thick arteries and veins that had evolved into the creature's wings, making them resemble the spokes of an enormous open umbrella. Winged beetles and tropical cicadas buzzed and clustered around the bat's face, with its rancid smells and specks of rotting carrion.

For a moment longer, the two sides – the bat and the men – stared at each other in disbelief.

The bat stood up on its hind legs and spread its wings to its full span – twenty, twenty-five feet! It began to screech with a volume that shook the entire platform. It launched itself violently into the air, flying straight at the dividing net.

Rasdyr, Jake and Dr Lefkovitz rushed back and away as the screaming bat crashed into the netting in front of them. The net stretched forward, its ropes extending until all slack was gone. The anchor branches strained and creaked like long, brittle fingers. It seemed certain the ropes would snap.

But they held.

The bat slammed its feet back down on to the

platform. Its head swivelled on its thick hairy neck. It hissed its outrage again as its stinking, scalding breath rolled toward the men. Its forelimbs boasted another set of talons that had atrophied into a comb of thick barbs. Like a rioting bird of prey, it screamed its ire through its dagger fangs.

It shuddered and rose up again. The ropes squeaked under the savage strain. But the bat was caught. Perplexed.

Furious.

Its talons shot forward and down, testing the ropes and planking for a weakness. Jake, his father and Rasdyr were stunned by the ferocity. The bat hurled itself against the netting like a crazed ram, its hooked claws reaching out to cut them. Savage them.

Kill and feed!

Jake checked the peak of the net, where the ropes drew to a nexus like the top of a circus tent.

The riverwalk platform quaked violently – but still the netting and wooden boards held. The bat seized the net in its teeth and shook it like an angry dog with a pull-toy. Leaves and fruit and beetles rained down from the highest domain of the canopy. All the small living things crawled and dropped off the edge, plummeting toward the jungle floor.

Jake and his father looked at each other.

'NOW!' his father shouted.

Rasdyr began to fire the drug-tipped darts. The first hit the bat's face. The second stuck in the bat's pug nose – and another hit the flesh above its left eye. The bat shrieked with renewed rage, and clawed at them until he scraped the darts off.

Dr Lefkovitz dropped down on his knees next to Rasdyr, grabbed another of the loaded blowpipes and helped fire off a second spray of darts. Rasdyr, too, fired again and again. The bat shook, screeched raucously, and bit wildly at the net that separated it from its attackers.

'I want the bat alive,' Dr Lefkovitz shouted. 'I need it *alive*.'

THE DEATH OF RASDYR

Jake, too, grabbed a blowpipe and managed to fire a drug-tipped dart into the bat's face. The bat stared maliciously at Jake and shrieked deafeningly. The violent fluttering and clawing of the bat was so alarming, even Rasdyr wasn't able to shoot straight. The darts began to miss their mark.

'Stop firing,' Dr Lefkovitz shouted. 'Don't provoke it anymore. Let the drug take effect.'

The bat quieted and backed away from the division net. It checked the trap entrance, clawed at it. But it was sealed, too.

The bat turned back to look at them. Rasdyr held another dart ready to fire, and moved closer to the net dividing the space.

'Be careful,' Dr Lefkovitz said.

The bat was standing up now. It was eerily quiet, checking every inch of the trap with its dark, mucus-rimmed eyes.

Rasdyr could see the darts were taking their toll. On various hunts, he had seen several tapirs and enraged jaguars succumb slowly to their power. The bat appeared to be drifting toward a sleep.

Jake relaxed and began to breathe deeply – fully – once more. He looked at Gizmo's screen, wanting to see how much clarity the electronic box was capable of. The screen easily rendered the shape and broad strokes of the creature. The image was recognizably the mutant bat, with its intense eyes and frightening teeth.

The bat appeared to be watching Jake and Gizmo now. It looked mesmerized, riveted, as if it were trying to figure out exactly what the device was. It seemed as if the monster clearly remembered the BEEP BEEP sound and the glow of its screen.

And recognized Jake.

Rasdyr used the distraction to move closer to the division net and the creature. He slowly picked up another of the drug-tipped darts, loaded a blowpipe, and held it aimed toward the bat's eyes. If the dart could strike the flesh of an eye, the drug would flow quickly to its brain – even make it collapse. From experience, he had learned the amount of the wildflower and eucalyptus sap that would cause a large animal to close its eyes and drop unconscious.

'Don't go too close,' Dr Lefkovitz warned Rasdyr.

But Rasdyr was already dangerously near the

division net. He raised the blowpipe into position. As he inhaled deeply to propel the dart through the long slender tube, the massive bat exploded into motion again. It came hurtling at the divider.

The force of the collision stretched the net farther than anyone had thought possible. The forelimb claws of the bat ripped through the net and grasped Rasdyr. The claws tore into Rasdyr's shoulders, and blood from an artery shot out like water from a shower hose. Jake and Dr Lefkovitz reached forward quickly. They each reflexively grabbed one of Rasdyr's arms, and tried to yank him back out of harm's way – but they were no match for the savage strength of the bat.

'EEEEH! EEEEEEEH!'

Rasdyr cried out in pain as the bat flexed its talons, digging them deep until they surrounded solid muscle tissue and bone. It pulled Rasdyr violently to its breast, at the same time leaping upward and digging the claws of its feet into the top of Rasdyr's midsection. Like a huge dark ostrich, it kicked its powerful legs downward. Rasdyr's whole abdomen burst open.

Instantly, Rasdyr was dead.

It was several moments before Jake and his father fully understood that they were holding the arms of a disemboweled corpse.

'Let him go,' Dr Lefkovitz shouted – to himself as well as Jake.

They released their grasp on Rasdyr's arms. The bat shrieked and tore farther through the net into the chamber. It let loose of Rasdyr's bloody body, and dropped down on to it. It tore at the dead face and neck and chest, not feeding or devouring. It used its teeth to slice and dismember.

Instinctively Jake threw open the volume switch on Gizmo.

BEEP BEEP BEEP.

The electronic blaring had confused the monster

on the night that it had grabbed Hanuma. Now, delirious with horror, Jake somehow hoped it would give him and his father the seconds they needed to escape.

His father had spun around and was hacking at the rear of the trap with his machete. The bat's rage was entirely focused on Jake and Gizmo now. Its nostrils dripped with a green ooze as it shook the netting and managed to thrust its cruel, snapping jaws further through the rip in the netting. Its flailing claws scooped and swung inches from Jake's legs.

As the bat rolled its head and screamed in a shaft of moonlight, its talons reached deep, pawing through the sad remains of what was Rasdyr. Suddenly, it grasped the palm-wood planks of the trap floor itself. It spread its wings with a power and turbulence that tore the division wide open, and it stepped through the entrails toward Jake.

The trap was a shattered spider web as Dr

Lefkovitz gave a final slash at the rear net. Its opening was wide enough now, and Jake crawled out as his father pulled the ropes apart with all his might. Jake's father was quick behind him – and they were running. A second later, the bat's head and wings crashed through the rupture, and it was after them.

'The sling,' Dr Lefkovitz called out.

Jake ran towards the centre platform. The sling to descend was waiting. It would hold both of them. Jake reached it. He leapt into it and held it against the railing, ready to launch.

'Hurry up,' he shouted to his father.

Dr Lefkovitz rushed toward him. The bat was crawling – racing – swiftly, half-flying after him. Jake held the sling open. For a moment, he met his father's terrified gaze and knew he had made another decision.

'Save yourself,' his father said.

'No!' Jake cried out.

Then his father was at the sling. The bat was coming fast. Jake turned the volume of Gizmo up still higher. The loud beeping was earsplitting, but it didn't slow the bat.

'Don't!' Jake said, as his father reached out for the sling release. It was too late. His father sent Jake and the sling descending toward the jungle floor. Horrified, Jake watched his father sidestep onto the north runway. The bat halted to see Jake and the retreating sling – then it made another, a crueller, decision.

There was shouting from the camp as the men realized that something had gone terribly wrong at the trap.

'The bat's after my dad!' Jake shouted as he reached the bottom.

Jake leapt out of the sling. He took off beneath the path of the north runway, straining to see up through a mesh of tropic evergreens and moonlight. The men, with cries of fear, raced along beside him.

There was a scream from above.

There came the sounds of a heavy weight crashing down from the canopy – something falling through the layers of delicate branches and strands of fleshy orchids and vines. There was the thud of a body hitting the sea of red clay and broad-leafs that were the jungle floor.

VENGEANCE

*F*rightened and shouting, the Indian men hacked their way through the jungle undergrowth and reached the fallen body first. Sorgno, the young man who could speak only broken English, grabbed Jake and led him to the spot. 'Your father. Hurt.'

Sorgno led Jake to where the group of men had gathered. Jake knew how far his father had fallen. He had heard the branches crack, breaking his father's fall as he smashed down through them.

The men stepped aside to make room for Jake. Some of the Indians had terror in their eyes; others had sorrow.

Jake walked to the centre of the group of men, and dropped down on his knees next to his father. His father was covered with bruises – tears in his skin. Capillaries on his arms had burst, and his eyes were closed. His face and hair were cloaked in blood, and his left leg stuck out in an impossible direction. A chunk of white bone protruded from the skin of his knee.

Jake saw his father's chest rise and fall, and heard his troubled breathing. Each breath was a hard wheezing. A struggle. He started coughing and a strand of blood dripped out the side of his mouth. Jake was afraid his father was dying in front of him.

But that mustn't be.

'Get a cot,' Jake yelled. He reinforced with

a mime of what was needed. 'Something flat. Hurry.'

Sorgno translated. Three of the men left for the lean-tos. Taking off his own shirt to use as a towel, Jake wiped the dirt and blood off his father's face. He took his father's hand and whispered in his ear, 'Don't worry, Dad – you'll be OK. We'll get you out of here.' Jake turned to Sorgno. 'We have to get his bone back inside,' Jake said. 'Set it as best we can.'

'I have done this,' Sorgno said. 'I can do it.'

Jake helped Sorgno straighten out his father's leg. He hadn't forgotten how the young Indian had left the wounded Hanuma alone – had left and allowed Hanuma to walk into the campfire.

The men returned with a cot. They all gently lifted Jake's father on to it and carried it like a stretcher to the main hut.

'My dad needs a doctor,' Jake said to Sorgno.

'He has to get down to the Fathers' village. To the missionaries. Muras needs treatment, too. They'll have to radio for a helicopter or my dad will die. I want your best rowers – the strongest river men – in their pirogues, and they've got to leave now.'

'We cannot leave on the river,' Sorgno said. 'They will be slaughtered like Hanuma and Dangari. We must carry Dr Lefkovitz and Muras through the jungle.'

'How long will that take?' Jake asked.

'Three days, maybe more.'

'My dad doesn't have three days,' Jake said, his patience running out. 'CAN'T YOU SEE HE'S DYING? DO YOU WANT ME TO PADDLE HIM DOWN THERE MYSELF? IS THAT WHAT I HAVE TO DO?' Jake shouted.

'The bat will get him,' Sorgno said. 'We will not go on the river.'

Jake's eyes filled with rage, and he shoved

Sorgno to the ground. Furiously, he drew back his fist trying to punch him, but Sorgno was faster. Stronger. He grabbed Jake's fists and stopped them from striking him. A darker, older Indian cried out from the doorway.

'Stop!' Muras said, barely able to stand. 'Sorgno is right. As long as the bat lives, your father and our people will never make it past the Dark Angel Falls.'

Sorgno let Jake get up.

Jake began to choke with anxiety and panic. Finally he had control again. 'If we all go downriver in the daytime, we'll be safe.'

'No,' Muras said. 'This bat will not be frightened of daytime. It will leave its darkness. Its roost in the canopy or cave in the river cliffs. Wherever it sleeps. Where it gains strength and readies itself.'

Sorgno translated for the men, and they began to cry out fearfully and shout protests in Murdaruci.

'The bat will come after us in the bright sun,' Sorgno told Jake. 'Blind as a bat is a lie. Bats can see with their eyes, too. It will not stop until we are all dead.'

'You believe that?' Jake asked.

'Yes.'

Jake saw that all the men were staring at him. He realized they were looking to him to convince them – to make the right decision. They were riveted on him as he had seen them look to his father and Hanuma.

'Then we're going to have to destroy it,' Jake said.

Sorgno told the men what was said. Again they reacted.

'They say that it will not die,' Sorgno said. 'We are the ones that will be killed.'

Dr Lefkovitz's eyes opened, and he cried out in pain. Jake crouched down at his side. 'They'll get you to the village,' Jake said. His father's eyes closed once more, and his breathing quickened.

Jake dipped a cloth in a cup of fresh water, and wet his father's lips. He knew his father was slipping fast.

'You'll all leave,' Jake said decisively to the men. 'I'll stay.'

Muras sat exhausted on the floor. He saw the hate and the ferocity in Jake's eyes. All the men knew that if they didn't do something, Dr Lefkovitz would die.

Jake said, 'The bat won't follow you if I make noise. If I keep the sounds of the camp going. I'll shout and yell, and make enough noise with Gizmo and my stereo. I'll blast it while you drift quietly away. I'll make a racket that'll make the bat think there are still dozens of us here. Besides, I'm the one it really hates now. Me and Gizmo.'

'If we leave you here, you will be dead,' Sorgno said.

'No,' Jake said, determined. 'It will be the bat who dies.'

The afternoon sun burned off the thick morning fog that had rolled from the river on to the banks. Muras had the men do everything that Jake wanted to prepare for his stand against the bat. They knew if they didn't get the men moving, they'd start defecting anyway.

Once Dr Lefkovitz had been safely strapped into a pirogue, the fears of the men reached a near-breaking point. Even Sorgno knew if they didn't all leave together, they'd panic and start taking off alone in a pirogue, or run away – two or three at a time – into the jungle. Divided, the small terrorized groups would certainly be stalked and killed.

Daylight was fleeing. Sorgno and Kiro, the strongest riverman left from the expedition, would take Dr Lefkovitz in the lead dugout. Jake had packed the medicines and Sorgno knew how to give an injection if his father went into shock.

The loading of the half-dozen dugouts was done quietly and under the cover of the mangrove trees at the left of the small beach. The loud sounds of the camp at work were simply just that – sounds. As the fingers of fog lifted for a moment, the only thing moving in the camp was the CD in Jake's stereo. With its volume on ten, it seemed like the whole camp was booming with its ordinary sounds of chopping and cooking and preparing for a night research trip into the canopy.

Jake gently and silently helped the men edge the last pirogue into the water. On board was Dr Lefkovitz, bundled up and strapped in like a mummy, but miraculously still alive.

Muras was the last to whisper to Jake. 'Be careful,' he whispered.

Jake nodded. He watched the men frozen still,

holding their paddles, as they began the drift along the downstream bank under the cover of a thicket of low, arching palms and a cover of buttress and stilt roots. The current began to move the cluster of pirogues silently, secretly, downriver.

Several of the men looked back at Jake. He saw the expressions on their faces, and decided it was a mixture of fear and profound sadness. It was as if they knew for certain that it would be the last time they'd ever see him alive.

Jake waited by the river for a long while after the boats had disappeared around the first bend. He listened to the noisy, coughing truck motor. He could see the silver flash of the large schools of piranha feeding on frogs and catfish along the far bank. The vibrations of the truck motor still kept them away from the camp beach.

As Jake walked back up the bank he hoped the blasting recorded sounds of the workers and rock music would be enough to keep the bat fooled that all was business as usual at the camp. Wherever it was, he knew it would be coming back as the sun set. It wouldn't take it long then to discover that he was all alone now.

Completely alone.

It was strange walking through the empty camp, but sounds from the truck motor and stereo comforted him. He found himself thinking, *You'll be OK, Dad. Even when the bat knows it's only me and Gizmo here, that'll probably be enough to keep it here for a while. Sorgno and Muras and the men will have you safely at the village ...*

Then he remembered the sight of his father bleeding and broken on the floor of the jungle, and he clenched his fists. He caught himself gasping, breathing fitfully. He knew his eyes were wide with fear – as if the bat were already attacking. As the full realization that he was alone hit him, he found himself stumbling, fighting for breath.

He looked down and saw the image of himself

reflected in the drinking trough. He stared, mesmerized. His hair and face were speckled with river mud. He brushed the dirt from his forehead, as if to make certain he was truly seeing himself. He saw tears in his eyes, and he knew there would be no time for anything like that.

He rubbed at his eyes, and a wave of realization rushed up and overwhelmed him. He turned and looked up into the failing light, at the treeline and labyrinth of the canopy, realizing that fate had given him enough strength for a fighting chance. Slowly, a look of vengeance and hatred crossed over his face and he continued his preparations to meet the bat.

NIGHT OF THE BAT

*T*he sun was setting fast along the Amazon. Clouds of mosquitoes rose from the riverbanks and giant aruanas leapt out of the water to catch baby lizards scurrying across vast stretches of giant lily pads.

In the last of the sunlight angling into the camp, Jake scraped the milky poison from a dozen of Rasdyr's scattered arrows and placed it in the ridges at the end of a single sharp blow-dart he'd whittled. He held the sticky sap over a bed of hot embers until the poison melted and fused solidly onto the tip.

By dusk, he had the last of his supplies out of the main hut and struggled to pull himself up by the sling. On this trip up into the canopy, he was loaded with a drum of gasoline and as many pots as he could tie on to the pulleys. He had had Sorgno and the other men bring up as much of the other equipment and materials as he could think of before they'd left downriver. They had beached a single pirogue, the smallest, for him.

If he needed it.

As Jake pulled himself higher, pain flared up from blisters on his hands. He looked out across the tops of the canopy sea and saw the last of the bright gold and purple clouds of the sky. Another evening he might have paused and looked longer at the sunset. But not tonight. Not now. He promised himself he'd watch it again soon with his dad. Yes, that was a fine thought. They'd be at a restaurant in Manaus, or Belem – or they'd be leaving on a jet back to New York. That thought gave him strength as he continued to pull himself up to the top.

In a promontory north of the camp – in a cave impossible to see from the ground – a pair of powerful, taloned feet held on to a rock face. As the sun sank beneath the horizon of jungle, the wings of the massive bat began to stir. Its eyelids moved and opened, revealing two black shining orbs. A moment more, and its wings stretched wide. Its feet loosened themselves from the rocky cave ceiling – and the bat dropped into flight.

Shrieking filled the air as thousands of smaller bats flew from the main cave in the cliff. Flying amongst them was what looked like a giant black condor. Its giant wings carried the creature along the river and towards the plumes of smoke from the camp in the distance.

It heard sounds. Sounds of men, and they made

its blood pulse and its stomach tremble with a hunger for *final blood*.

By the light from the string of bulbs surrounding the centre platform, Jake opened the five-gallon container and poured the gasoline over the wooden octagon. It was the one cleared area where the lush canopy itself wouldn't have a chance of burning. He tossed the empty drum over the side. Seconds later, he heard it hit the jungle floor.

Jake grabbed two of Magyar's largest cooking pots, a twenty-five gallon soup kettle and a large aluminium frying pan. He thought of Magyar, and what the bat had done to him, and an anger filled his chest. He began to bang the pan lid on the bottom of the kettle. Hard. Crazily. The racket echoed through the night sky and along the river.

Come and get me. Come ...

Not far away, the giant bat separated from the

main swarm of smaller chiroptera and swooped down, skimming along the tops of the trees. It flew over nests of marmosets, which it normally would have dropped in on for prey. But tonight was different. Tonight the giant bat had a craving no howling monkey or plump anteater could satisfy.

It wanted the child of the leader. Of the invader. It wanted the boy ...

The bat heard the noises of the camp and crashing of metal in the canopy. In a moment more, the creature's sonar zeroed in on what it was looking for.

Jake, standing in the platform's light.

Jake saw the massive, dark wingspan against the moonlight. The bat was heading right for him. He tossed the pots down on to the platform and waited.

When the bat was less than a hundred yards away, Jake took matches from his pocket and tried to strike one. It broke against the box. He looked up to see the bat was above him now, shrieking like a massive bird of prey. With his hand shaking, Jake grabbed another match and scraped it against the box. Its tip burst into a small flame. He heard the swishing of the bat's wings as he tossed the match into a narrow trail of gasoline leading to the soaked platform.

Jake ducked as the bat swooped lower, uncurling its claws and opening its mouth. Suddenly, the gasoline trail hit the main pool and exploded into a lagoon of fire. The bat veered away, but the flames surrounded it. Jake heard its first cry of surprise, which turned into earsplitting shrieks of agony.

The bat flew out of the fire, its abdomen and wings singed. The moisture on its snout boiled and the tips of its wings were charred. The bat was wounded, angrier than ever as it flew toward him. He dived as the bat's talons dragged right over him.

Jake ran away from the fire on to the shadowy riverwalk. He cried out as he glanced back. The bat was still after him. He tripped, rolled up on to his feet, and took off, slogging through the veil of vines and along moss-covered railings. He spun and stumbled again, this time turning his ankle, then scuttling like a crab on to the rotting planking over the river.

The bat made a wide circle. It had no problem finding Jake sprinting away. It extended the giant claws of its feet. As the creature bore down on him, Jake made a flying leap off the darkened end of the walkway and grabbed on to a rope wrapped around the trunk of a balsa tree.

The bat slowed its flight and fluttered in a circle around the girth of the tree. In the darkness, it picked up a human silhouette on its sonar and flew right for it. Its front claws and jaws clamped down on to it, and it began to rip the form apart.

It hadn't noticed the metal stripping and wires that connected the effigy to the dangling bulb sockets.

The creature screeched as a bolt of electricity shot off from the wired effigy. The bat's muscles contracted and released, as the pulsing hot voltage burned into it. It threw itself backwards and away from the rigged effigy. The bat fluttered and floundered down into the shadows of the walkway. Jake swung around from the other side of the tree, a machete in his hand.

As he charged at the dazed bat, the smell of rotting flesh mixed with the stench of the creature's burned hair filled Jake's nostrils. He saw lesions and blood coming from the ruptured skin of the bat's wings and ears. As Jake closed on the bat, he raised the machete above the creature's wing.

With an explosive squawk, the bat sprang to life. Its eyes glared right up at Jake, and its wings shot forward, smashing into his arm. The machete flew out of Jake's hand and over the edge of the walkway. Jake tottered and grabbed the handrail. As Jake steadied himself, he felt a pain in his arm. The bat had carved a slice into his wrist. Holding onto the cut, Jake took off running again. Ahead of him was a dead end and behind him was the bat.

Furious, the bat took flight.

At the end of the walkway, Jake quickly slid himself out along one of the dozen ropes which spider-webbed across the river. He reached a second effigy he had set, one that hung this time in the midst of a dozen of them so it looked like a mobile of life-size men. Jake looked back and grabbed for his pre-set stash of Gizmo and the power belt. He fastened the belt around his waist and strapped Gizmo's screen on to his forehead.

The moon was blotted out by clouds and the night fog. Jake was in total blackness now, a strong wind blowing across the Amazon. He could see nothing with his eyes, but Gizmo's beep-and-retrieve system was coming in clear. He was able to feel the images – the sounds created on his forehead. He was aware of the effigy turning too fast, of the images blurring. He had to remember what it was like to concentrate, as he'd trained himself for so many months, to see like the blind – 'see' the sound pictures of terror.

FINAL STALKING

He heard the noises of the bat – its terrible shrieking – and the creature's sonar generation. Its sounds confused the images on Gizmo, and Jake struggled to make sense of everything. He looked down toward the water far below. He knew even if he fell he probably wouldn't survive.

The bat swung into the dead end of the walkway and spotted a human silhouette. It flew for it and smashed it with its mighty claws. But it smashed an effigy and the bat knew the difference between crushing wood and crushing human flesh.

It sent its sonar out across the spider-webbing ropes and picked up human silhouettes hanging from a half-dozen branches that stretched out over the river. The monstrosity flew to the next effigy and grabbed it, smashing it into splinters. It flew to the next and smashed that into pieces, too.

From behind the effigy he clung to, Jake saw the bat systematically make its way among the branches, destroying effigy after effigy. He looked out to the netting he'd stretched and set as a trap above the river.

The giant bat smashed an effigy only a few branches away.

Jake took the blowpipe from his holster. He carefully removed the poison dart from its hollow bamboo shield and slid it into the tip of the blowpipe. The bat landed on the effigy next to

Jake, and he watched its finger-like spiked claws pulverize the wood and branches.

Jake brought the blowpipe to his mouth. The giant bat flew to the branch above him, and lowered itself to his effigy. As the creature spun the effigy around, it was surprised to see a figure clinging to it.

Summoning all his breath, Jake aimed and blew into the blowpipe. The dart flew out from the blowpipe and sunk into the tender, hairy underbelly of the bat. Shrieking, the bat flailed at itself – finally knocking the dart loose.

Jake's hands shot up to the pulley line from which his effigy hung. He yanked himself free of the effigy, and dangled. A second later and he was propelling himself, hand over hand, farther out over the river. As his momentum carried him, he wanted the bat to see the glow of Gizmo. He wanted the killer to follow him now with great speed.

This time there was nowhere to hide. The bat swung in and headed for Jake. It knew it had him. The bat raised its wings and thrust its claws forward.

Jake was under the net he'd rigged at the centre of the river. He turned up the BEEP BEEP of Gizmo. He wanted the bat to fly into place beneath the rope web. The poison might kill the bat, but it would take much too long – and Jake had counted on this final surprise.

The bat was screeching, outraged, circling around Jake.

'FLY OVER HERE AND GET ME,' Jake yelled. 'I'M WAITING FOR YOU. COME ON, YOU BIG, COWARDLY CHICKEN.'

The bat flew straight at him. The creature came fast, and Jake yanked the trigger vine. He'd planned there would be time to pull himself clear – to be out from under the net as it fell like a cloak onto the creature's head and wings ...

But his hands were slippery with sweat. His grip failed, and now the net was falling on to him *and the bat*. The night mist had moved on a breath of wind, and Jake kicked out at the bat, but the wide, weighted net was already covering both of them. It trapped the two of them, and they began to fall.

Jake yelled.

Like a torn parachute, the fluttering wings of the shrieking bat slowed their fall, but they hit the surface of the river with a great splash. Jake felt the pain on his back, like he'd landed very wrong off a high diving board. The bat's wings, ebony and streaked with blood, loomed over him. He and the bat began to go under.

They both shuddered and gasped desperately for air, struggling to free themselves from the net. Their cries were chilling – frenzied – and Jake was certain they'd drown. For a stark and eternal second, Jake and the bat's eyes met, and in that moment – in a curious and strange way – Jake knew he had always had a destiny with this nightmare. Perhaps it wouldn't have been deep in a primordial jungle. But this moment would have come. Somehow. Somewhere. In the mirror of the bat's eyes, Jake glimpsed his father's dream of him – the design of who he was supposed to be.

Now – suddenly! – the bat was biting fiercely at the net, fighting to tear it with its teeth and talons. Jake shouted, wanting only to keep clear of the gnashing teeth. He threw off Gizmo and the power belt, and tried to dive under the net – to find a way out by going deeper.

The trap held firm, and when Jake surfaced, the moonlight was dazzling and he could see the bat had managed to put a long tear in the net. He grabbed for the opening and emerged free into the current. Jake swam toward the sound of the truck motor – towards the camp – and didn't look back until he was closing on the shore. His feet touched the muddy bottom.

Exhausted, he made his way slowly into the shallows. When he was closer, he thought to look behind him. There was no sign of the net or the bat. A rejoicing began to fill his heart and his total being. The creature was dead and he was alive. He began to compose a kind of prayer, to shape his thoughts of amazement that he had survived.

The killer bat was gone. The ordeal was over ...

He emerged from the water near the truck chassis and its running engine. He was thankful its gasoline hadn't run out, but he didn't want to think about that. His mind needed to think of nothing. It needed to rest and eat and sleep and—

SPLASH.

A terrible sound – the noise of water being

splashed violently. Jake spun around. The bat, near shore, had burst upward from the surface like a phoenix. It rose high, so high that Jake thought it would be airborne, as a missile in a sea launch. But the bat hadn't enough strength yet to fly. It fell back on to the surface. The horror was clawing, floundering toward him. With each stab forward of its wings, it gained strength.

Jake thought he might run. He would try to make it to the main hut. But the cough of the truck engine resonated in his brain. Instinctively, his hand shot out and shut off the gas feed – the lifeline to the engine – and the motor stopped.

He looked across to the opposite shore. There was the flickering of silver fish as they easily – speedily! – followed the blood trail of the bat. Seconds later, the bat began to shriek in agony. The fish had reached it. The water around the bat began to boil scarlet. The creature desperately

– pathetically – swung its wings upward in a last attempt at flight. Dozens of frenzied piranha had already fastened themselves to its skin.

More piranha came, as if the whole river was filled with the hungry fish. The bat's shrieks grew louder and angrier and, finally – its cries were hopeless. Its winged forearms became skeletal, its skull stripped of flesh – and the creature sank, slowly disappearing into the blackness of the river.

For a while Jake rested on the bank of the camp. The moon was high in the sky, and at the horizon the first glow of dawn began to creep into the sky. By daylight it was clear the river was rising, and he would have to leave in the last pirogue. A family of sea otters came downstream in the first wave of the flooding. They stopped and played in the slowly drowning mangrove roots, the younger ones sliding in the last crest of the muddy bank. The largest of the otters hunted for fish in the new shallows.

Soon, strength returned to Jake, and he began to plan the trip home – the trip downstream – before the entire camp would be beneath the swelling river. As he launched himself in the pirogue, he could sense in his heart that his father was safe. Somewhere safe. The men would have made it to the village. An army helicopter would have come. His father could even be at the hospital in Manaus.

But there would be many of his father's men – his workers – still at the village when Jake drifted out of the river mist in the small dugout. He knew the workers would be watching for him. They would tell the village. Jake would be embraced by them, and there would be a gathering. There would be a fresh roast boar, and something cold to drink. He would be invited to sit with the men around a campfire. They would sit and listen as he told them about the end of the night of the bat.

For more gruesome tales by Paul Zindel,
look out for

RATS

THE FESTERING

*H*is first day back from the Fourth of July
vacation, Leroy Sabiesiak knew he'd get some
good target practice with the rats in Area 17.
'Garbage Siberia,' he muttered to himself as he
mounted his bulldozer. He checked the stubble
on his leathery face, made certain his flask of

vodka was tucked into the hip pocket of his overalls, and left the main Sanitation Depot at 7.05 a.m. He headed the bulldozer out past the asphalt cover of the dump to what was left of the open garbage.

He was glad the dump was nearly sealed. He'd been working there from the beginning, before it had the fancy name of 'The Staten Island Landfill'. Over two decades of breathing the reeking garbage was enough. In a few weeks he'd be retired, start collecting on a fat pension with health and dental care, and it'd be time to dream.

He kept his eye out for rats as he edged the bulldozer along the south rim of the asphalt. Macy's and the Pep Boys tyre store were across the highway in the mall. On his right was one of the new black mountains of tar. 'I'm gonna miss ya,' he yelled at the smothered dump. 'Yeah, I'll miss ya.'

RATS

'Hi, guys,' Leroy called out as he drove the bulldozer on to the freshly-dumped garbage and saw the first few rats of the day scurrying across the top of a heap of meat scraps. 'I'm gonna see a lot of ya by the farm today!' he said, stopping to grab his BB gun and fire off a few shots. 'It's gonna be my little farewell present to ya all!' Leroy knew he would have gone nuts if he hadn't made a game out of the rats from the beginning. He could hit a rat on the run at fifty feet. Hit it right in the face. About that, he was very proud.

Leroy had noticed the increase in rats over the last few weeks. He'd shot hundreds of them, but there were so many, he'd taken to bringing along City-issue packets of poison, which he'd dip in peanut butter.

'Ya love peanut butter, don't ya, fellahs?' Leroy shouted at the rats. He knew they loved peanut butter more than anything else. Their next favourites were sardines and beer! 'Love ya poison with a little fish and brew, don't ya!' He could always tell when a rat had got a good dose, because the poison would react with the rats' digestive juices and puff them up with gas. The rats would swell up to twice their size before they died a horrible painful death.

Ehhhhh. Ehhh.

He'd hear them dying. In their last hour they'd stagger over the top of the dump like drunk balloons. Leroy loved pumping their bloated bodies full of BBs. He'd hit them dead in their eyes.

Leroy spotted a fresh pile of dumped appliances and furniture. He left the bulldozer motor running and got down with the BB gun to check things out. 'Lookin' for a good refrigerator,' he mumbled. 'Wouldn't mind findin' a decent cuttin' board, either.' Half his house was furnished with stuff he'd found at the dump, including a 21-inch mahogany TV with Picture-In-Picture and a SWAP button.

BING. BING.

He got off a few good shots at the bloated rats on top of the body of a dead collie somebody had thrown out with the trash. People had no respect any more when it came to what was legal garbage and what wasn't. He plodded further away from the bulldozer and pulled his boots up as he sank deeper into the garbage.

For a while he forgot about the time and enjoyed shooting every rat he could. When he turned to start back to the bulldozer, he noticed half a dozen big rats sitting on a distant ridge of garbage.

BING. BING.

He fired at them one after the other. He hit several of them right in the head. Dark red fluid gushed out of their mouths and ears. He was about fifty feet from the bulldozer and went after another line of fat rats that appeared on the highest ridge.

'I'll shoot ya in ya ears!' Leroy yelled at them. 'In ya ears and ya bellies. I'll hit ya where it hurts!'

He spotted a swollen mother rat trying to salvage her nest of straw and threads and bottle caps. In a moment he was standing over her, pumping her mouth full of lead pellets. He saw her naked, furless babies, barely able to move, and he shot each of them, too.

He was laughing when the first rat bit him.

He hadn't seen it coming at all. He knew there was a line of them on a side ridge, but suddenly one of the rats had turned and raced across the top of the garbage. Before Leroy could stop it, the rat was in the air. It landed on his shoulder, digging its claws into his collar bone and sinking its chisel-shaped front teeth into his back.

'Whoa!' Leroy yelled. 'What are ya doin'? What do ya think ya doin'?'

Leroy reached around and grabbed the rat by

its wet, oily fur. He tore it off him along with a strip of his own skin, punched the rat, and hurled it away across the dump. For a few moments he tried to laugh, but he was too surprised by the attack. Confused. He couldn't think of anything funny to tell himself. That was when he felt something he'd never felt before.

Something like . . .

Like fear.

It was the sight of a hundred – two hundred! – rats that came over the ridge as a unit.

'Ya keep away from me!' he shouted as the rats inched closer. His voice was empty now. Hollow. He felt his arms begin to shake, and his belly drew into a chilled, rock-hard knot.

CHIRRRRR. CHIRRR.

The rats made low sounds like some sort of fowl or sea birds. Large, half-muted ocean birds. As they advanced, the garbage made its own crackling noises from under their weight. His tongue grew thick and dry, and his eyes started to tear and burn. His instincts told him to get out of there.

Fast.

Get back to the bulldozer.

Leroy started off, but his boots sank deeper. He got less than ten feet before he noticed several dozen of the rats had ducked into the garbage and were writhing beneath the debris in front of him. Thick brown bodies, some as large as a foot, slithered like shining fish beneath the surface of a muddy pond. They closed and rose swiftly to the surface. A dozen rats began to bite at Leroy's legs as he spun around swinging the butt of the BB rifle.

'Ya get away from me! Ya get away!'

Several more larger rodents from the ridge were airborne now. They landed as a single clump on Leroy's neck, biting him deeply. The rats hung on tight like a living, gnawing scarf as he screamed.

Twenty – thirty! – rats were biting at his legs now, ripping open veins and arteries as they tripped him.

'Nooooooo!' Leroy cried, trying to crawl the distance to the bulldozer.